What Did He Have to Ooze?

She sang the sequence through a couple of times, her voice low and carefully modulated, then tilted her head, her eyes still closed, and began singing something else, her "Spring Hunting Song."

"Out spirit-hunting again?"

She nodded without interrupting her music.

Then her expression changed, became one of surprise and alarm. I dropped the washcloth and took up my short sword to stand beside her. Perhaps the steel would be of no use against whatever it was she felt . . . but I felt better for having it.

Her eyes opened and she stared past me at the door. I whirled.

Coming through the door was a man, if man he could be called. From the raven's-wings tattoos on his shoulders and his rough beard and hair, he was a mountain man. But he was gray—of skin as well as of hair and beard, a continuous tone like some grades of pretty building stone—and stark naked.

And when I say he was coming through the door, I do not mean that he was walking through an open doorway. The door stood closed and bolted as I'd left it. He oozed through it like a sticky jelly, parts of him clinging to the wood as he tried to pull free of it; more of him flowed into the room, especially by way of the gaps between the planks that made up the door. He gazed upon my wife with an expression of avarice. Or perhaps it was just longing magnified until it was something inhuman. . . .

THE BARD'S TALE SERIES

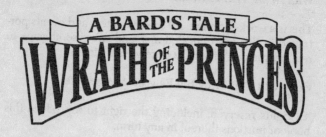

A BARD'S TALE
WRATH OF THE PRINCES

HOLLY LISLE
AARON ALLSTON

WRATH OF THE PRINCES

Copyright © 1997 by Bill Fawcett & Associates

A Baen Books Original

The Bard's Tale characters and descriptions are the sole property of Electronic Arts and are used by permission. The Bard's Tale is a registered trademark of Electronic Arts.

Baen Publishing Enterprises
P.O. Box 1403
Riverdale, NY 10471

ISBN: 0-671-87771-2

Cover art by Ken Tunell

First printing, March 1997

Distributed by Simon & Schuster
1230 Avenue of the Americas
New York, NY 10020

Typeset by Windhaven Press, Auburn, NH
Printed in the United States of America

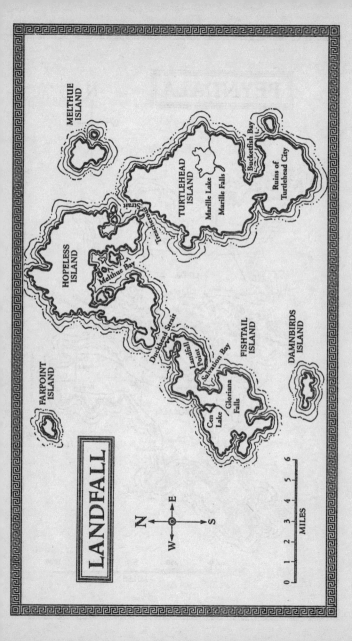

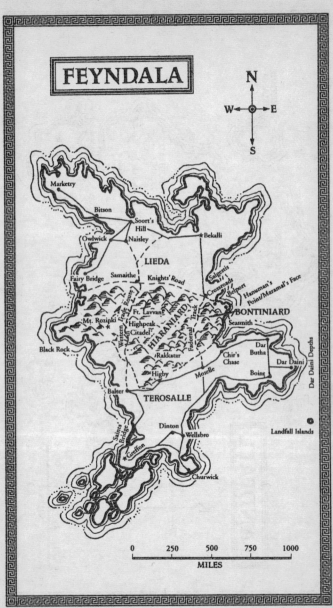

FEYNDALA

N
W—◇—E
S

Marketry

Bitson

Soort's Hill

Owlwick
Naisley
Bekalli

LIEDA

Fairy Bridge Samaithe Knights' Road

Salgentis
Crossroads
Belport
Hanuman's Point/Maramal's Face

Western Trade Route
Ft. Lavvan
Highpeak
Citadel
Mt. Rozipki
HIARANIARD
Federual Track
BONTINIARD
Seasmith

Black Rock
Rakkatar
Chir's Chase
Dar Butha
Dar Daini

Higby
Moselle
Boint

Balter
TEROSALLE

Dar Daini Depths

Saints' Bridge
Dinton Wellsbro
Landfall Islands

Greffon

Churwick

0   250   500   750   1000

MILES

Prologue

From the Journal of the Honorable Kin Underbridge, Judge of Lieda and Byriver

I don't know why they call it the "dead of night." If anything, everything seems more alive at that hour.

I stood on a hilltop overlooking the village of Byriver. I was cold, in spite of my size and my well-patched garments of leather and wool. Hard, cold winds, among the last fingers of winter's grip, hammered me from the distant polar south. Past the hills to the south, I could see the moonlight glinting on the ocean.

"I'm ready," said Halleyne, my bride-to-be.

Even the pallid light of a moon just reaching fullness set off her beauty—emphasized her delicate build and fiery spirit and the proud carriage that made her seem taller than she was— for if you count great height as an asset in a woman, then height was among her few deficits. I will report that I am not one who does. To me she was perfect, and at that moment, I thought her most perfect of all. Several weeks back on the main island had erased from her the signs of the winter of deprivation she and the other rebels had endured. Our baby had not yet made itself evident in her figure, and would not for some weeks to come. She'd wrapped up in a long cloak but, facing into the wind, could not keep her hood up; her fine hair, golden-blond by day, but silvery in the moonlight, snapped to and fro in the buffeting wind.

I stood behind to catch her in case the wind pushed her clean off her feet.

Her shoulders rose as she took a deep breath. Then she began to sing. The wind rushed around her so strong and gusty that a few steps from her I would have heard nothing.

She sang in Terosai, her native language, a more melodic and subtle tongue than my own Liedan. Within a few bars, I recognized her song.

"The Ride to Hanuman's Point." It dated to one of the many times in centuries past when her homeland, Terosalle, was at war with Lieda. It told the story of Terosai prince Nimiatran dar Lere, whose military skills were sore-needed in battle at precisely the same time his wife lay deathly ill, in need of his presence to sustain her.

What did Nimiatran choose? This was a patriotic song. He chose the battle, of course, and won it handily. Then he mounted the freshest horse he could find and raced off across the bodies of the slain toward his home, knowing he could never reach it in time.

Although history says Nimiatran's wife was weak from childbirth and survived because of a doctor's skill, the song tells the story differently. The prince's horse begins galloping with eerie smoothness of gait. The prince essays a look to the side and discovers that he is a tower's height in the air and rising fast, borne aloft by magical powers. He is carried home to Hanuman's Point faster than a hunting hawk can fly. Within an hour he stands beside his wife's bed and she recovers, all a gift of the gods because the prince did his duty to queen and country.

Such songs annoy me. A man ought to make hard choices knowing that sacrifice means loss; he should not be convinced by stirring tunes that sacrifice means the gods will fix everything if his love of country is sufficiently strong. But for all that I dislike such songs, and this song in particular, Halleyne had chosen her music well: it told of men and magical forces cooperating, and in every chorus it mentioned the place that Halleyne and I wanted to go—Hanuman's Point on the east coast of the continent of Feyndala.

As she reached the part where Prince Nimiatran sights his mansion far below, the winds around us suddenly died down; Halleyne's voice wavered on her lyric, showing her surprise. The air became utterly still as she sang of the prince's landing, rushing to the side of his lady, her smiling and being miraculously healed—

And Halleyne's next noise was not the last refrain, but a squeak of surprise as the wind howled again and she was lifted straight up into the air.

I grabbed at her, got both arms around her legs, and was suddenly battered by harsh, cold gusts. My weight stopped Halleyne's upward flight, but the buffeting wind-spirit nearly yanked me off my feet.

"No!" I heard her cry. "Not me! You may not have me!"

I let my legs go limp, trying to drag her back to the ground by sheer weight, but the force that held her aloft was too strong; she merely bobbed up and down. I swore at the wind-spirit that had her, promising, if it carried her away, a dire revenge I doubtless had no way to bring about.

Halleyne was shouting "Cave, cave, cave!" like a babbling child. Then whatever held her suddenly let go. She fell atop me, bearing me to the ground. I seized her around the waist before her attacker could reclaim her and wrest her away.

The winds returned to normal. Halleyne's skin felt icy to my touch. She gasped for breath—I reluctantly loosed my grip on her so that she could inhale. And finally she turned and smiled down at me.

"I suppose it worked," I said.

"Yes. A south wind spirit. It has agreed to carry us from this place. To the west, against the prevailing winds, against its true nature. But it wants a reward."

I blinked at her. "You? It can go to the hell of tired, used-up breezes."

She laughed; there was a nervous catch to it. "I was its first choice. Can wind-spirits mate with mortals? That was the impression I had of its intent."

"They did in legends," I said irritably, and sat up, still holding her. "And many flighty heroes were conceived that way. I infer that there was a second choice."

"Yes. It wants a cave. A cave that will make music when the winds fly through."

"Truly?" I thought about it. I'd once spent years as companion to an engineer. "That could be done. Baffles and constrictions. It would be making tunnels into something like woodwinds."

"I'm glad it can be done, because I told it that it would be done, within the year. And two days hence, it will come back for us and take us home."

"Home." I held her close. "Halleyne—"

"Not again."

"Yes, again. Did you ask if the spirit could conduct others home while you, we, stayed here?"

"No."

"It means going to sea while you are with child."

"Yes. I think you've grasped the situation, Kin." But her expression softened, removing the sting from what might have been harsher words. "On the mainland, we'll find a proper midwife or doctor who can ease the birth. And we *must* find an experienced mage who can tell us if our child is to be . . ." She wavered on the word.

What word would she have chosen? *Malformed? Possessed? Evil?*

This is my second volume chronicling the fates of the Landfall survivors. In the fullness of time, it may be that the volumes are not to be found together, so I am duty-bound to mention here what has gone before.

In the twenty-second year of the reign of King Jerno of Lieda, Princess Thaliara of Terosalle was affianced to Prince Jernin of Lieda, Jerno's first legitimate son. Captain Buyan, an officer of the army, and Jerno's favorite illegitimate son, was sent to Terosalle to fetch her forth. But Buyan's expedition disappeared. Each side claimed that the other had captured the royal offspring for ransom, and war began.

By the thirty-fourth year of Jerno's reign, and the twelfth year of the war, both nations were sick of fighting. Jerno had lost his three legitimate heirs; I, a general's son with little potential for a military career, had been companion to two of the princes and was now the king's valet. Lia, Queen of Terosalle, had lost both her daughter and her next heir, a niece. With nothing but more pain to be gained from further warfare, King Jerno sent for Sheroit dar Bontine, a famous negotiator from the mountains between the nations, to bring about a treaty of peace.

Sheroit arranged for the last stages of the negotiation to take place where neither side had any advantage: on the waters off Hanuman's Point, a disputed territory on the east coast. It was there I met Halleyne, who was scribe to Queen Lia, and was my counterpart in that she served as the queen's eyes, ears, and (sometimes) brain.

Once the treaties were signed, disaster struck. Wind-spirits summoned by magic drove the two warships and dar Bontine's barge out to sea. The barge survived only a few minutes, with dar Bontine riding out the storm aboard the Liedan ship. Both warships were destroyed on the rocks and reefs of Landfall—our name for a misbegotten circle of islands far from any shipping lanes.

Having recently discovered peace, the leaders of two nations abandoned it almost immediately. The Liedans built one village, the Terosai another, almost adjacent. The rulers squabbled constantly, Jerno showing sign of increasing madness, Lia growing ever more vile-tempered and unjust. While the lower classes worked hard to construct huts and build up stores of food to last us through the upcoming winter season, the nobles of both nations lived as well as anyone could on the fruits of labor not their own.

Real trouble began at the outset of winter. The Terosai Bard, a lovely lady by the name of Shallia, friend and teacher of Halleyne, left the Terosai to join the Liedans. Her wish was to marry Nerrin Axer, a Liedan commoner, and King Jerno granted that wish. But when the day of the wedding came, he revealed another plan. Having lost all his heirs to war, and being married to a queen who was past childbearing age and still in the land he and the rest of the castaways had lost, he decided to set aside his wife in absentia. He appointed me to a judge's position and commanded me to marry him to the same Lady Shallia, against her wishes.

Having little choice, I did. But immediately afterwards I began conspiring with Lady Halleyne to separate Jerno from Shallia and return the Bard to her husband of choice. Halleyne tried to keep the spirits of the unwilling bride high, that she not do herself harm, and together they practiced music and Bardic magic; it was then that Halleyne discovered she too had a knack for magic, the gift to summon spirits.

Soon after, revolt erupted. Jenina Morlin, former second mate of the Liedan ship and, by attrition, senior naval officer among the Liedans on Landfall, led a combined force of Liedans and Terosai, mostly commoners, to slay both rulers.

With the help of the remaining loyalists and those who had some affection for me, I checked the revolt and banished the revolutionaries from Fishtail Island to the more distant Turtlehead

Island. Unknown to me, they carried Halleyne with them; she had been injured in the revolt, but it was reported to me that she was dead.

Soon after that, Sheroit dar Bontine and his ally, the Terosai apprentice mage Teuper dar Hiaro, took me aside and made a confession. They were part of the conspiracy that stranded us. Just before the great storm, Teuper had slain the royal wizards who might have given warning of the winds to come. He and Sheroit had tried to flee the ships in time, but the winds had come early and kept them among us. But now, having stolen the surviving ship's boat, they were preparing to leave; though the winds and seas were normally too dangerous for such a small vessel to survive the return home, Teuper had struck a deal with a wind-spirit. The wind would bear them home.

Then Sheroit, Teuper, and another confederate tried to kill me; their confession had been to amuse them as they watched my face and to distract me while their confederate crept up on me. Their attempt to slay me failed and I killed the third conspirator. Still, they escaped.

I led a revolution of my own, telling the increasingly addled King Jerno that I would rule while his mind was ill. This he accepted, and at my request he set aside his marriage to Shallia so she could rejoin her true intended. That was one of the few happinesses winter accorded me.

The revolutionaries on Turtlehead Island had an even worse time of it. One of their number was a man named Daneeth Po. He became vassal of strange spirits that lay beneath the island—beneath all these islands. The creature we called Snake-Mother—an ancient being, whether goddess or malignant spirit it is hard to say, whose name was long lost to men—was trying to rouse herself from a sleep of centuries. At the start of the spring thaw, her serpents and Daneeth Po attempted to bind the revolutionaries to their cause by mystic means. I traveled to Turtlehead at that time, seeking to learn whether Halleyne still lived . . . and, briefly, Halleyne and I, and two other castaways named Raldan and Leiala, were Daneeth Po's prisoners in the buried temple of Snake-Mother.

It was there, in that less than agreeable circumstance, that Halleyne and I first made love. There, too, Raldan and Leiala, obeying Daneeth Po's directives, mated. All of us were suffering some effects from the spirit-magic of Snake-Mother.

We learned later that the chambers we occupied were Snake-Mother's temple of fertility. Learned later that both Halleyne and Leiala had conceived that day, more than likely under the influence of the goddess' magic. Learned later that Daneeth Po imagined that the unborn children belonged to Snake-Mother. We escaped, but knowledge of Daneeth Po's words filled us with dread of the future.

As Daneeth's serpent allies laid siege to Jenina, Halleyne, and the other revolutionaries, I made my way back to Fishtail and called for a rescue expedition. Days later, a ramshackle navy of rafts put in at Turtlehead and carried the revolutionaries to safety . . . and, not incidentally, slew Daneeth Po. In the course of this, the Bard-in-training Shallia demonstrated the powers of a full Bard and forced Snake-Mother back into slumber . . . for the time being.

That is where matters stood in the days after the early thaws of spring. Now Halleyne had succeeded in duplicating Teuper's feat: summoning a wind-spirit and striking a bargain with it. Our future, which had so many times seemed a road buried by avalanche, was clearing once again.

Chapter One

I stood on the deck of the *Arrow*, the flagship of the navy of Byriver, and heaved her sea anchor overboard. All of which sounds more glorious than it actually was.

The *Arrow* was a canoe. Granted, she was a big canoe, hollowed from a mighty tree. She was an outrigger, the type of canoe islanders make; wooden beams held a smaller, unhollowed log out at a distance from and parallel to the canoe body, the better to keep the craft stable in rough seas. Our canoe even possessed a small mast that could be stepped when the winds were favorable.

And our sea anchor was a large wooden bucket tied to a length of rope which was then tied off to a peg on our bow. It was modest, but it would provide some drag in the water and keep our bow facing into the wind—west, toward Fishtail Island, in this case. I waited until the line completely deployed and the bucket bit into the water, straightening us, then I turned to check on my companions.

On the bench nearest the mast's step sat Shallia Kantrin. A lovely lady, tall and lean, with dark hair and a broad smile that was still sometimes

11

melancholy, she had only a moon ago entered a goddess' temple and used her Bardic magic to push the goddess back into sleep. Anywhere else in the world, this would have accorded her the rank of full Bard, but here there were no ranking Bards to see and report the deed. She would have to remain an apprentice for some time to come. She wore a woolen overtunic and breeches of the hide of the seal-like melthues, for though the winds were out of the west instead of the polar south, the air was still cold.

A step beyond her, on the next bench, was my own lady-love, Halleyne. It still surprised me, the way my heart thudded whenever I caught sight of her. She was a dainty beauty, an unlikely match for as clumsily bearlike a man as I am, with fair hair worn long and blue eyes that could be warm as a pool in a royal estate, or cold and sharp as broken ice. When first I'd met her, she was in the habit of marring her beauty with makeup, the better to escape the petty jealousy of her queen, but it was the keenness of her wit that first drew me to her, long before I saw her true face. Today, less suited than some of us to the cool weather, she was well-bundled in lined melthue-hide garments and wrapped up in a heavy woolen cloak.

At the stern of our mighty naval vessel stood Jenina Morlin, senior naval officer among our Liedan shipwreck survivors. Tall and rangy, she had a manner as dark as her hair and eyes While no one would call her pretty, she was certainly striking. Prideful and unpredictable, she shared a past with me that logic insisted should have led to a different present than the one we shared. I had once bashed her with a club; she had once tried to kill me with an improvised spear. We were now allies, nearly friends. She dressed as though it were much later in the spring; she went barefoot, in patched sailor's breeches and a ragged vest that left her arms bare, and even so the wind did not seem to affect her.

It occurred to me belatedly that I was aboard ship with three women, all of whom were crucial to the success of today's mission, while my own usefulness was limited to heaving a bucket overboard. I sighed and wondered if the world of manly men, in which my father and uncles seemed to have lifelong memberships, had vanished while I wasn't looking. I shouted to Jenina, "Sea anchor deployed."

She waved to indicate she'd heard, then shouted, "Best be at it, ladies."

Halleyne and Shallia gave her a rueful look and stood; Halleyne reluctantly emerged from her cloak with Shallia's lute in hand, and at Shallia's nod began to play.

I recognized the tune. An old lullaby; Shallia and Halleyne had sung it to the snake-goddess in the first part of our foray into her temple. Then Shallia began to sing—but not words; she sang pure single notes in harmony with the soothing tune. Her eyes, unlike Halleyne's, were closed, and I imagined her pulling back from her perceptions of the world so she could gauge the effects of her song on her distant, incomprehensible audience.

Then her song changed. Her notes remained a counterpoint to Halleyne's playing, but no longer were an agreeable harmony; they became haunting, eerie tones. I pulled my own cloak tighter

around me. Her song slowed, and Halleyne
fumbled with her playing just a moment as she
became accustomed to the new meter.

Halleyne's playing faltered again a moment later
as air burbled up from the depths of the water. It
was as though a hundred swimmers beneath our
canoe suddenly drowned and gave up the air in their
lungs; bubbles came to the surface a dozen paces
in all directions all around us. But this was not air
from human lungs; I caught a whiff of its stench as
the wind blew it past us. It was sulfurous and vile.

There was only one such eruption, and a
moment later both the choppy sea and the air
were normal again.

Shallia's discordant song continued to the end
of what would have been the last of the traditional
lyrics; as she neared it, she signaled to Halleyne
that they would not continue, and my lady-love
finished off the lullaby with an uncharacteristically
mournful set of notes. Then Shallia opened her
eyes—eyes that looked more troubled than when
she'd closed them.

"The news," I said, "must not be good."

She shook her head.

We resumed our benches and oars and got back
to the job of rowing. We could have stepped the
mast and let Jenina's command of sail take us
in, but we were all working hard to make sure
we were fit for the expedition to come. As we
rowed, with the breath her exertions left to her,
Shallia explained.

"Snake-Mother is directly beneath us," she said.
She spoke over her shoulder; Halleyne and I had
the benches behind her, Jenina the bench in front.
"In the earth under the sea floor."

"I thought she was under Turtlehead Island," I said.

"No. And yes." She looked a little confused. "Each time I've done this, I've made my way closer to where she actually lies. And I see a little deeper into her sleeping mind. To her thinking, there is no Turtlehead; there is only one island, *the* island, directly above her. An island of fire and rumbling."

"A volcano?" Halleyne asked. "I've heard of them."

"I've seen one," Jenina said over her shoulder. "An island far to the east. The islanders talked of it giving off fire like a sorcerer gone mad and throwing rock, ash, and poison into the air."

"Which must have happened here," Shallia said. "Long ago. It killed all the people . . . and split the island into many. Turtlehead, Fishtail, Hopeless, and all the smaller ones. But she lies under what was once the highest point."

"And is now the lowest," I said. "But at least she's still sleeping."

"For now," Shallia said. But she didn't sound hopeful. "Kin, she wants to awaken. She's slowly waking up. I did a little good today, and will do as much as I can to soothe her back into sleep. But it won't work forever."

It wasn't just the cold of the air that sent a chill through me. If our experiences of a moon ago were any indication, the Snake-Mother did not dislike humans . . . so long as they were properly infected with the little spirits carried in the venom of her servant snakes, the so-called Gloriana vipers, which flourished on Turtlehead Island. The effects of this infusion of serpent spirit tended to make its victims subject to the Snake-Mother's wishes . . . and eventually altered the victims. "How long do we have?"

"I don't know. Days. Moons, perhaps. She's lazy. Just becoming aware that she wants to wake, but not impatient about it. With no humans here for so long, she had no reason to want to wake, and she's still sleeping deeply enough that she's slow to feel any urgency. But I think the more aware she becomes, the harder it will be for me to do any good." Shallia looked dejected. "I'm the mouse whispering lullabies to the awakening cat."

"Don't be sad. You've done quite well. You'll give us all the time we need." I spoke with confidence I didn't quite feel. I was certain some of us could escape soon enough to avoid the Snake-Mother's attentions . . . but maybe not all of us. "We'll talk more in council," I said. "We'll settle on the crew and other things then."

So we put our effort to the oars and kept our subsequent thoughts to ourselves.

It was a long row in to Fishtail Island, our home. We beached the *Arrow* in Salvation Bay, the east-facing bay where we washed ashore those many moons ago, and I made sure that Viriat Axer, former bodyguard to the king, came on duty to guard the canoe. Then we all retired to our huts to rest before the council meeting.

In my hut, on my own cot, though I lay with my lady-love's arms wrapped around me, the sleep I fell into was troubled and unrestful.

Hours later, we assembled in the "throne room" of King Jerno's hut. This was a large, drafty area attached to the back of the king's hut; at least it possessed walls and a roof.

The representative council I'd summoned for the meeting would, under other circumstances, have been considered quite prestigious.

Already on hand when Halleyne and I arrived was King Jerno. A massive man, he was as tall as any bodyguard who had ever served him and as muscular, but a year ago all the muscle was concealed under a years-long accumulation of fat. In the last few moons he had lost his last son to war, had been shipwrecked with his longtime enemy Queen Lia, had taken a new wife by force and then been forced to relinquish her, had lost his mind . . . and had, I believe, at long last regained it. Now, moons after our exile began, he'd lost a lot of the unneeded weight and in form seemed much more kingly, for all that he was wearing ragged, patched remnants of royal garments. He sat on the crude wooden throne at the head of the table, but I found it significant that he'd removed the pile of earth that had once elevated the throne a foot or so above the ground. Behind him stood Garris Bricker, his sole remaining bodyguard.

"Welcome, Judge Kin, Lady Halleyne," Jerno said. "You are free to enter the royal presence." He added that with a touch of irony; he well knew that I currently had more control over this "kingdom" of Byriver than he did.

Next to arrive were Shallia and her husband-to-be, Nerrin Axer, Viriat's brother. Nerrin, a one-time dresser for the king, had worked with Shallia shortly after our shipwreck on the absurd committee we'd assembled to map and name everything on these islands. He and Shallia had won one another's hearts and pledged to marry. When King Jerno married her against her will, he made an enemy of Nerrin, so it was no look of kind friendship that Nerrin leveled on the king as they entered the throne chamber. But Shallia had been restored to him and he was bound by a promise he'd made me not to kill Jerno. A hunter, he was well supplied with melthue hide, and most of his garments, in good repair though hard-worn, were made of the stuff. Shallia sat by Halleyne and Nerrin by her, so the four of us took up almost one long side of the table. Shallia and Halleyne immediately fell to talking about a choice of songs for tomorrow's feast.

Next was Jenina Morlin, representing the navy of Byriver—Byriver being the parts of these islands under the theoretical control of King Jerno. She sat directly opposite me, looking bored, and struck up no conversation.

Then came Maydellan Ha, royal physician of the queen of Terosalle. He was the only one of his kind on these islands, that is to say a true dwarf, from the Terosai mountain-city of Rakkatar. Even by dwarven standards he was homely, with a bent nose and scarred features; he once told me that he'd been a champion fist-fighter in his youth, and I was inclined to believe him. He wore his beard long and unkempt, had spectacles to improve eyesight he'd ruined by reading too much, and wore breeches and tunic heavily patched with bits of scrap cloth representing a dozen different colors. "Good evening," he said, and took the seat opposite Nerrin. "Is everyone well?"

King Jerno snorted. "It will do you no good

to drum up business, Doctor Ha," he said. "No one has money to pay you."

"Ah," said the doctor. "Well, then, I pronounce you all cured."

Last to arrive by several minutes, to nobody's surprise, was Lia dar Kothia Surdosti, the Gloriana Majeste of Terosalle—as the queens of Terosalle style themselves. A small woman, she had been beautiful in her youth and was striking even today, but could not admit that she was as far removed from thirty as a thirty-year-old is from infancy, and was heavily floured with makeup to hide the fact. (How she had managed to bring a many-moons supply of makeup onto the island I was not sure; perhaps, like Halleyne, she'd learned to make more from resources on the island.) She wore a gold-hued queenly garment that was largely intact in spite of our many moons of exile. Her bodyguard, Beran dar Petris, a dark man smaller than our Viriat Axer but reputed to be as good a fighter, bore her wooden throne into the room and set it up at the table end opposite Jerno, then he and Zilona dar Machias, the queen's lady-in-waiting, stationed themselves behind the throne as she sat. In the most modulated form of her shrill voice, the queen announced, "We may begin."

Before King Jerno could make his routine protest that it was not her place to say so, I cut in: "We certainly may, since it is well past the time we should. Lords and ladies, we have a simple task to accomplish tonight, so it shouldn't take us much past dawn." There was a ripple of amusement at my faint joke. "We have to decide on the final roster for the expedition home. We

can accommodate a small crew, minimum four—
which is what it takes to move our flagship at
any perceptible rate when there is no wind to
bear us—and maximum eight. And, of course, we
have to meet the representational needs of the
kingdoms involved." Which, I didn't need add, was
where most of the debate was likely to originate.

"Who do you have confirmed for the crew
now?" asked Queen Lia.

"The Lady Halleyne dar Dero and myself," I
said. "Halleyne is the only one of us who can
convince a spirit of the winds to convey us back
to Feyndala. And if she goes, I go. Jenina Morlin
is also assigned to the crew; even with a wind
at our beck and call, we'll need some of the crew
to be knowledgeable sailors."

The king murmured, "Already an admirable mix
of Liedan and Terosai interests."

Queen Lia made a face as though she intended
to spit on him from the length of the table. "Oh,
certainly. Two Liedans and a woman who has once
betrayed Terosalle already."

"Beyond that," I said, in hopes of forestalling
an argument, "the crew is not yet established."

"Where will you make landfall, Terosalle or
Lieda?" the queen asked.

"That's outside the scope of this meeting," I
said. "The composition of the crew and other
circumstances will decide that."

"No, that has to be decided first. It has to be
Terosalle."

"If that's the thing you insist on talking about
first," I said, "you can return when we have that
meeting."

She glared, but she knew from experience that

she couldn't bully me into changing my agenda, so she fell silent.

"The purpose of this trip is to arrange a rescue expedition; restoring rightful rulers to their thrones is secondary," I said. "We've already agreed not to rescue Liedans at the expense of Terosai, or vice versa. This means we'll beach where we first sight land—or signal the first ship we come across. We'll find out what the situation is at home, and go where we'll find it easiest to arrange the rescue. No other consideration has any bearing on what the expedition as a whole does."

Lia sighed. "Agreed," she said. "But Terosalle is still much closer."

"Yes. But across a much deadlier stretch of sea, the dar Daini Depths." Waters so storm-tossed and treacherous—and, it is said, inhabited by malevolent sea-beasts—that even the mightiest naval vessels took time-eating detours close to the coast rather than sail across them "If we can pursuade our wind-spirit to take us due north and then west, we should reach Hanuman's Point, which suits us as a neutral starting place."

"I think I should go," said Jerno.

That caught everyone's attention. "Not advisable," I said.

Jerno smiled. "Actually, I think it's very advisable. I have to acknowledge that my reign here has not been a complete success—"

That brought a bitter laugh from Nerrin Axer. To his credit, the king did not respond, even with a scowl.

Jerno continued, "—to the extent that my influence here is negligible. During my illness, Judge Kin assumed control of my portion of these islands and has, for reasons I must recognize as good ones, not relinquished it. It may make more sense for me to wait here for the rescue ship you will dispatch . . . but I can do no good here, and might be of use on the expedition."

Queen Lia looked offended. "You just want a head start in resuming your throne. Then you can attack Lieda before I return."

"No." Then Jerno turned to me. "Judge Kin, I am making no demands of you. But I want to be part of this expedition, and I have certain qualities to offer as . . . as a crewman. Even if my throne has been assumed, I know many who would remain loyal to me and could offer us shelter, aid, and a rescue ship to return here. I am strong. In my youth I was a hard worker; when we were building the rafts to go to Turtlehead, I became one again."

"You're afraid of the open sea," I said, as gently as I could.

He shook his head. "When the sea was just an opportunity to drown, I was afraid of it. Now that it's a road home, I welcome it. I've spent time on the rafts and on the *Arrow*. I don't think that old fear is still with me."

"Then I'll consider it."

"You will not!" That was Queen Lia, of course, ready to see a threat in every circumstance that even hinted that it might not go in the direction of her choosing. "You cannot put him on the crew unless you have someone of similar rank from the Terosai. I'm the only one, and I'm not stupid enough to go."

"I'll decide that," I answered with a fair approximation of my usual calm.

Halleyne whispered in my ear, "You'll decide whether he'll go, or whether she's stupid?" I had to tighten my face to avoid an inappropriate grin.

"Well, you'll have to represent me," Queen Lia said. She was looking at Halleyne.

My lady's expression turned to one of surprise. "What?"

"Absolutely! You *have* to represent Terosalle on this expedition. Make sure all Terosai interests are upheld." The queen gave her a look of resigned, somewhat contemptuous acceptance. "So. Halleyne dar Dero, it is my unhappy duty to appoint you *thalahai* of the realm of Terosalle and charge you with the task of representing my interests back in Feyndala."

We fell silent. I worked my mouth, but there were no words in it. The Terosai rank of *thalahai* was much like the Liedan rank of knight, a formal type of nobility; unlike our knighthood, it is inheritable, and almost always granted in association with lands and royal friendship.

Halleyne found her words before I found mine. "You denounce me as traitor at this table, and a moment later pronounce me a noblewoman?"

The queen's mouth turned down at the corners. "Oh, it's distasteful to me. But you're going, you're Terosai, and I know you'll do as I wish. Like a well-trained dog, you're sure to discharge any task given to you."

"Queen Lia," I said, "this is not the place or time to fling insults." I was surprised at how deep my voice had gone.

The queen merely smiled at me, an expression that under other circumstances might have been charming. "Don't be absurd, Judge Underbridge.

That was a compliment. The obedience of dogs is their most noble trait."

Halleyne, her own voice under tight control, said, "I have no interest in—and certainly no skill in—making sure your interests are represented."

The queen nodded. "A woman on her wedding tour wants no distractions, I know. But you have never renounced your Terosai name, or heritage, or family. For all you're marrying an enemy, you are still Terosai, and I still may make demands of you. Or do you wish to renounce all allegiance to Terosalle?"

That hung in the air between them—that, and the queen's mention of Halleyne's family. If the queen did return home and reassume her throne, it would be very bad for the dar Deros if Halleyne had earned the queen's hatred.

"Of course not," Halleyne said.

"Good." The queen smiled. "Then if you give me a piece of paper from your book of calligraphy—one of your precious blank pages—I will draft your document of entitlement."

Good wherever your reign is still acknowledged, I thought. *Good only if we manage to reseat you on your throne.* The queen might have been nasty, but she was not stupid.

The king smiled. "I propose you draft two additional copies, one for each of our royal archives. I will gladly add my signature as witness. That will be the first document we both have signed since our peace accord was struck. And it will be the oldest with both our hands set to it, since the treaties did not survive the shipwreck."

The queen's face lost a little of its malicious cheer, but she gave him a short nod.

"We have our minimum crew of four, then," I said. "Halleyne, myself, Jenina, King Jerno."

Nerrin Axer said, "Most of the people on the island want to go."

"Naturally," I said. "Now pare away those who have no pertinent skills to offer us, those whose temperaments are unsuited to spending several days on angry waters in a small boat, those who will be unnerved by the magical sending Halleyne will be making, those who are too physically frail for the journey, those who might stab any of the crewmen already chosen; who does that leave?"

"Not many," Nerrin said. "Viriat wants to go."

I nodded. "He'd be a good choice. Big, strong, a good fighter, should we run into trouble. Objections?"

There were none, not even from Queen Lia, who kept a small, proprietary smile turned on my lady-love.

Chapter Two

The next day was a little warmer. This was a good sign. Halleyne said that it would be best for us to set off when the warm northern winds were coming into play but before the cold southern ones vanished utterly. Were she a more powerful Bardic sorceress, she could perhaps command one against its will, even making a western wind blow us from west to east, but for now, she had to beg favors of a wind that had nothing better to do.

I dressed in my finest. Mind you, after moons on this island, almost nothing we owned was fine. But my cloak, still in good condition, had been washed and wind-dried, and I'd cleaned and polished the leather of my boots and belt. In anticipation of this event, Halleyne, so adept with hues and chemicals, had dyed my best tunic and pants so the numerous patches were hard to see.

I went to see Shallia.

I found her in the hut she shared with Nerrin Axer. She stood tall, beautiful as any bride-to-be, wearing the sea-green dress that was one of the few items of formal women's wear to survive the shipwreck undamaged. It was, owing to color and condition, the default bridal gown for the ladies of the island, and Shallia stood straight and uncomfortable while Halleyne pinned it here and there, with crude pins made of bone, to better conform it to her contours.

Not for me to intrude long on the last-minute preparations; I merely stuck my head in the doorway. "All's well?"

Shallia gave me a smile and a nod. Halleyne gave me a sharper look. "All but the constant parade of visitors and well-wishers."

"Ah. Well, by decree of my office, I'll have them all beheaded, starting with myself." I ducked out again.

No need to check on Nerrin Axer. He was doubtless with his brother Viriat, who would have him in place and on time or die trying. I headed to the beach.

This was the beach of Salvation Bay, where we'd first been thrown up on the shore after the shipwreck. Many of the castaways avoided it for that reason—because of the memories it evoked. Memories of being carried there by waves while clinging to wreckage of what had been a great warship, half-mad with fear of death by drowning. Of staggering, exhausted, onto cold sands, tripping over the cold, water-bloated bodies of men and women who had only hours ago been friends.

That was one reason I'd insisted the ceremony be here. It represented the disaster that had overtaken us, to be sure . . . but now, with the *Arrow* dragged up on the sands in full sight of the ceremony circle, it would be a symbol of our now-reasonable hope for rescue.

Also, some of my reasons were practical. It was

a wide, pretty beach, where the entire population
of the island could comfortably assemble, where
fire pits could be dug for the ceremonial feast
to follow. They had been; I could see melthues
roasting on spits, the distinctive lumps of clay-
wrapped fish baking among the coals.

Many of the castaways were already on hand;
some had friendly greetings for me. Others,
followers of Jenina who had a harder time than
she in forgiving me for banishing them, kept their
distance.

I found the spot I thought commanded the best
view of the *Arrow* and the fire pits, halfway
between them. There I dug the marriage circle,
dragging my heel through the sand to make a
boundary about five paces in diameter. In these
modern times, the marriage circle—a ritual border
drawn between the happy couple and any person
or force that might wish them ill—is not always
used, but I thought today's celebrants would
appreciate it.

Then I rehearsed the ceremony under my
breath, over and over, knowing that it would do
no good, and that when the time came I would
forget every third word.

The bride's party arrived first. Shallia was radiant
in her green, which showed no sign of having
fit her like a potato bag earlier in the day, and
Halleyne was no less beautiful and joyous in a
garment pieced together from survivors' dresses
and well-dyed in a festive red. Behind them trailed
well-wishers and friends, mostly Liedans. Jenina
was among them.

As they arrived, many of the celebrants waiting
on the beach began to move in toward the

wedding circle; all, however, followed custom and remained outside it. There was much laughter and hushed conversation from the bride's party, with some of the jolliness—to guess from the glances being cast—pertaining to me; I maintained my judgely decorum and ignored it all.

Minutes later the groom and his brother arrived. Nerrin and Viriat, both of them hunters through most of the winter, had had access to a fair amount of melthue hide and wore almost-matching outfits of leather breeches, jackets, and cloaks; for all that the garments were well-worn, the Axer brothers looked dashing and identically intent.

I gave the crowd a look. King Jerno and his bodyguard were arriving—to my considerable surprise, in the company of Queen Lia and her retinue. I'd thought Lia would surely stay clear of the weddings of ladies who had, in her estimation, betrayed her, but she marched forward in expressionless dignity. Both she and Jerno, perhaps sensitive to the fact that they would not be the most favored guests here, stayed to the rear of the gathered crowd.

But their presence was a propitious sign. A wedding witnessed by two royals was not likely ever to be disputed, no matter where it was conducted.

I looked at Shallia and she gave me a little nod. I looked to Nerrin and he did likewise. So I threw up my hands—a theatrical gesture that billowed my cloak up and back over my shoulders, attracting everyone's eye—and began.

"Shallia Kantrin," I said, "born Shallia dar Kantrin, step forward."

She did, with sure steps that suited her happy expression. Behind her came Garris Bricker. That was a surprise; the custom of the Guardsmen had not entirely vanished away from modern weddings, but I had not expected the bodyguard of Shallia's former husband to take the role today. I glanced at King Jerno; he gave me a little shrug.

"Nerrin Axer, step forward."

And the groom did, followed by his brother Viriat acting as his Guardsman; that was no surprise at all. The Guardsmen, of course, are charged with the task of staying alert for the arrival of anyone who might offer a ritual challenge to the marriage; should such a person show up, the Guardsmen were to beat him nearly to death and throw him into the street. Or, in our case, into the bay. So long as death did not result, any such beating was approved by tradition; under these circumstances, even the royals would not be exempt.

Suddenly I understood Garris' presence. King Jerno had to have offered Garris' services to Shallia. A way of saying, "See, by my own decree, not even I can interfere this time." An interesting gesture from the man who had forcibly wed Shallia the last time she had tried to marry Nerrin.

I looked between bride and groom. Both of them beamed, showing not one fraction of the nervousness I felt; they were looking at one another, not at me. "We are here," I said, "in clear view of the gods, and may they look upon us and bless us.

"It is customary at such times to speak of the obligations husbands and wives owe one another. But I think no such instruction is necessary here."

That caught Shallia's attention and she glanced at me, her smile partly concealing sudden intensity as she tried to get at the meaning of my words. She and Nerrin had been living together in the manner of wife and husband since King Jerno had divorced her, just as Halleyne and I had since our escape from Turtlehead Island. My words might have been a jab at her and Nerrin for anticipating their wedded state, but I could see she correctly guessed that I'd merely thrown out a hook to reel in her attention. She gave me a brief mock-scowl.

"Shallia Kantrin, do you consent to be wed to this man?"

And that was politics, even in the midst of such a happy ceremony. In a proper wedding, the judge or priest always first addresses the higher-ranking member of the couple. When both are of equal rank, in Liedan weddings the man is first addressed, and in Terosai weddings the woman. But Shallia and Nerrin were not equal; she had some minor Terosai title that granted her little but the right to be called "Lady," and Nerrin had nothing. Too, all the people of the island knew that it was her Bardic expertise that had quieted the Snake-Mother a moon ago; no one would have stood for me to call Nerrin's name before hers.

"Yes," she said.

"Nerrin Axer—"

"Yes." He looked startled; the word had just popped out. A few in the crowd chuckled at his discomfiture.

"Nerrin Axer, do you consent to be wed to this lady?"

He took a deep breath, gave his lady-love a

look of apology for marring the ceremony, and again said, "Yes."

"Your hands, please."

He, standing to her right, extended his left hand, and she her right; they crossed their wrists and held hands in the traditional manner.

From my belt I took a lengthy thong of hide and began wrapping it around their wrists as I spoke. "Earth-Mother, grant them fruitfulness. Rock-Lord, grant them strength." I used appellations instead of proper names because in this distant land I did not know whether the Feyndalan names would be appropriate. "Bright Nurse, grant blessings upon their children. Gilded Lord, grant them bounty."

Around and around the thong went, and then I began tying a particularly difficult knot I'd learned from some of the sailors. Shallia, seeing this, gave me another scowl—the knot would be horrid to untie, and tradition proscribed cutting it, for that would be bad luck. But tradition also said that the priest or judge tying a difficult knot was also asserting confidence in the success of the marriage, and it is that I was conveying.

"Wind-Lord," I said, "grant him might and fury when it is called for, and grant her always the stirring of breath in her flute, the stirring of wind to strum her harp-strings. By my right as judge of Lieda and Byriver, under the eyes of the gods, under the eyes of mighty rulers, I declare the union of marriage between Shallia and Nerrin. Let happiness remain between them forever!"

The assembly erupted in cheers. Shallia and Nerrin fell into such an embrace and kiss I felt I could not have separated them by inserting an oar between them and prying. I shooed them and their Guardsmen out of the marriage circle so they might receive the embraces and back-clappings of all the attendees.

Halleyne emerged from the crowd and fell into my arms. "Properly done," she said.

"I didn't forget anything?"

"Not a word. Of course, you did forget to lace your boots."

I actually looked. Of course, my boots were laced up tight. I scowled at my lady. "You would take advantage of my moment of distraction."

"When is a better time?"

Unobtrusively, King Jerno stepped into the marriage circle. With his heel, he began retracing the circle I had dragged in the sand. A moment later, he called out, "Lords and ladies, we are not done here; another duty stands between us and our feast."

My heart thudded. I put a hand over it and pressed as though to slow it down.

"Kin Underbridge," he said, "Judge of Lieda and Byriver, step forward."

I did, my feet moving seemingly without any direction from me. I heard someone heavy fall in step behind me and knew it was Viriat, serving his double duty for the day.

"Halleyne dar Dero, *thalahai* of Terosalle, step forward."

Again, politics, and a clever stroke by Jerno. He'd summoned Halleyne by the title Queen Lia had only given her the other day . . . and had done so in Lia's presence. This was as important a confirmation of Halleyne's new title as any certificate, assuming the queen did not speak up in objection. And she did not.

I was oblivious to this at the time, though. All I knew was that Halleyne appeared at my right side. I turned to beam at her—with all the wit and presence of mind, I imagine, of one of the inbred champion bulls of Naisley Province—and saw that Jenina stood behind her, charged with the duty of the Guardswoman. I smiled at Halleyne.

And then there was some talking. I remember answering, but, lost in the mesmerizing blue of Halleyne's eyes, I'm not sure what I said. Halleyne spoke, too, briefly. Something went on with my wrist, but I couldn't be bothered to pay attention.

Finally, after far too long a wait, there was distant cheering, and Halleyne came into my embrace and I kissed her. After a while, strong hands tugged at me, but I didn't want to let go, so I kept hold of my bride while we were drawn out of the marriage circle and into the crowd. I felt claps of congratulation on my back.

"Is it done?" I asked Halleyne.

She laughed. "Weren't you paying attention?"

"You made that impossible." My wrist was linked to hers by melthue hide tied in a knot easily as fiendish and complex as the one I'd used for Shallia and Nerrin. "Oh, damn the man."

"Get to work on it, husband, or we'll have a hard time at the feast. And afterwards."

At that feast, surrounded by well-wishers, dining on the best the island had to offer, and in the hours afterward, in our hut in Halleyne's loving company, I was as happy as I'd been in years, knowing the last pure and relaxed joy that I was to experience for moons.

✧   ✧   ✧

In the deepest hour of night, I was awakened by someone—something—scratching at the door to my hut.

I sat up in the darkness, felt warmth stir beside me. Halleyne's hand found mine. With my other hand I found my favorite knife and stage-whispered, "Who's there?"

Such a situation called for a whisper. Someone who braved the icy nighttime winds of early spring had something to tell me in confidence; I'd help no one by bellowing out a greeting and waking half the village.

The whisper came back, "Zilona."

The Queen's lady-in-waiting. I rose, the knife still in hand but held out of sight in a reverse grip, and unbarred the door.

She stood alone, her slight frame bundled up in a jacket and cloak crafted out of uncomfortable sailcloth. The moon gave me a glimpse of a sliver of her face: one eye, the bridge of her nose, one corner of her mouth. I allowed her entrance.

Light flared: Halleyne, striking flint and steel to ignite one of the ship's lamps salvaged from the shipwreck. She muted the light so the interior of my hut was but dimly illuminated.

"What brings you out at this bleak hour, Zilona?" I asked.

She looked between us. "I want to go with you."

"On our expedition? Don't be daft. Didn't you spend most of the time we were anchored off Hanuman Point green with seasickness?"

She nodded. "But I have to go. The queen—"

I felt sympathy for her. Halleyne had made it clear to me that Queen Lia was a far worse employer than King Jerno had been, irrational at the best of times instead of at the worst. But I had to limit our crew to the minimum number of people who could do the expedition some good. "Can you draw an oar?"

"No."

"Do you have powerful friends at home who might aid us?"

"No." She shook her head, smiling slightly, seemingly unconcerned.

"So what do you offer us by way of skills?"

Her smile grew broader. She moved to our cot and, from beneath the cloak, drew a threadbare cloth bag. She fumbled a little with the knot, then spilled the bag's contents over our blanket.

Jewels. Rings, brooches, earrings, necklaces, medallions, anklets, bracelets, all of gold, most studded with precious gems, a double handful of them.

I'll admit I stared. I could sell such a mass for a fortune, buy a house, live the rest of my life as a country squire.

I heard Halleyne gasp. "The queen's jewels," she said.

Zilona nodded. "But which ones?"

Halleyne took a moment to reply. "The lower-shelf jewels."

I looked between them. "What do you mean?"

Halleyne explained. "Queen Lia has a small casket of her jewels, salvaged from the *Thunderer*. In it are two little shelves that may be lifted out. In the top shelf she keeps her favorite pieces; on the shelf below, those she wears less often."

"So you've stolen half the queen's jewels."

"Yes." Zilona shrugged. "Half the ones she has on the island, anyway. A small portion of the ones she owns. Listen, I am no fool. When you return to Feyndala, you don't know what you will find. Both Terosalle and Lieda may be ruled by those who'd prefer for Jerno and Herself to stay gone, or dead. Am I right?"

"You are."

"You may have no resources to draw on. No one willing to support you. This is wealth. It can take you where simple good intentions can't. All I ask in return for it is a place on your boat."

"And, I imagine, acceptance in Lieda. You won't be able to return to Terosalle."

"That would be nice."

I looked at Halleyne. She looked very uncomfortable, but returned my glance and said, "She's right, Kin."

I scooped the jewels back into the bag and handed it to Zilona. "No. Take these back to your mistress' casket."

Her face showed her shock; she could not speak.

Irritably, I shoved my feet into my boots and drew my cloak around me. "I'll walk you back to Queen Lia's hut. And while we're about it, I'll tell you what I think of your thieving ways and your self-serving little plans."

Chapter Three

The day of our departure was auspiciously clear and mild. Though it was a workday, most of the island's population assembled on the northern promontory of land, facing Duckhead Strait; it was there I'd had the *Arrow* relocated for our departure.

Across the strait lay Hopeless Island, a jumbled rock upon which only the stubbornest plants found purchase. I remembered both island and strait with little pleasure. It was on Hopeless that I'd found the body of Admiral dar Ostaferion, the experienced seaman who might have been able to help us fashion a seaworthy boat and escape this place; upon the island where numberless Gloriana vipers nested. It was across the strait, then frozen by the winter cold, that Jenina's rebels had fled, bearing with them the unconscious form of Halleyne, while I wrestled with the lie I'd been told that she had been killed.

Workers, Terosai and Liedan laboring together without visible rancor, loaded our little craft. We had bundles of food, bladders of water, well-sealed leather cases containing letters in the hands of King Jerno and Queen Lia—some for their courts, if the governments were still loyal to them, and some to old friends who would remain loyal regardless of what the governments did.

Jenina and Jerno stood beside the bow of the *Arrow* where it lay beached. Viriat Axer was still loading our provisions; he gave me a little nod as he moved back for a new load. Halleyne stood alone, a little to one side, her expression perturbed. I took her hand.

"Kin, I'm not sure you did the right thing with Zilona."

I looked where she was staring and saw Queen Lia and Zilona, the latter wan and tense, toward the back of the crowd. "I did what I thought was right."

"I understand that. But it just doesn't seem like you. You have no love of Herself. It would not distress you to steal her jewels to fund us. If Jerno and Lia are both out of power, we'll need what that wealth could bring us."

"Trust me, Halleyne. I made the right choice."

She sighed and squeezed my hand. "I do. I just wish."

Shallia and Nerrin joined us for embraces and well-wishes. Minutes later, Viriat gently loaded the last of our provisions, a large sailcloth bag, into the canoe. I sighed and met my obligation as the expedition's speech maker.

"Attend, attend," I called. "Since this is the last time you have to listen to me for weeks or moons, you could do me the courtesy of listening well." That got me a laugh. "I have no great words of import today. We leave today that we might return soon . . . and then all leave this wretched place forever." That got me cheers. "Keep us in

your thoughts and prayers. Perhaps, if the gods
have these little islands on their maps, they will
convey your blessings to us. Good-bye."

Another spate of cheers; then, when I put my
shoulder to the *Arrow* to shove her back in the
water, men and women we were leaving joined me
in the effort. In moments the outrigger was afloat
and I, drenched from the waist down, scrambled
into my bench, the last crewman aboard.

Minutes later, as we paddled to get clear of
the island shallows, we could still hear the calls
of those who remained behind. I gave them a
cheery cry of "Get back to work!" but doubted
they could hear me. Finally, when the last
stragglers on the beach were tiny and indistinct
in the distance, we truly began.

We stepped the mast and Jenina raised our little
sail, adjusting it to make full use of a true southern
wind. We spent several long minutes making sure
that all our provisions were well lashed in place,
Viriat taking special care with the last bag he'd
loaded aboard. And when all that was ready we
turned to my bride.

She gave us a weak smile. "It's much more
comforting under the sun, with so many friends
around," she said hopefully. Then she closed her
eyes, took a deep breath, and began to sing.

It was "The Ride to Hanuman's Point" again,
of course. I could tell at once that she'd been
practicing it when I was not around; her notes
were purer, more practiced, with no sign that she
lacked for instrumental accompaniment. I could
see that the Terosai lyrics were lost on Jenina,
but Viriat and Jerno turned wry grins at the
choice of music.

She got to the end—or so I thought; but then there was another stanza, one she or Shallia must have added, in which Prince Nimiatran dar Lere speaks the praises of the forces that had borne him home. It was an obvious sop to the ego of the wind Halleyne was calling; but I hoped that what was manipulativeness easily understood by humans would be interpreted as due praise by a wind-spirit.

Halleyne reached the new end of her song and started in again, this time varying the chorus with the keening, mournful sort of notes found among the clansmen of the mountains between Terosalle and Lieda. I'd heard this sort of haunting music from traveling minstrels but was for the first time aware of how much it sounded like the wind passing through a cave-riddled cliff side.

Then the wind struck us.

In all my thoughts about this day, I'd imagined that the wind-spirit would helpfully sidle up behind us, give us an unseen nod and a wink, and set us into motion like a group of workmen pushing a haywagon.

Instead, we were blasted from the side by a howling, screaming wall of wind. The sail snapped out to full extension, threatening to tear free of its ropes. I saw the mast bend under the impact. The canoe tilted to starboard as the outrigger to port lifted clear of the water.

Halleyne was blown toward the cold, threatening sea, a look of surprise and alarm on her face, but I caught her before she took that plummet. Jerno and Viriat stumbled. Jenina, still holding onto a trailing rope from the sail, kept her grip as she was swung off her feet; by sheer strength she kept herself from being hurled over the side.

Struggling for balance, we saw the outrigger rise two full paces above the water's surface; then it slapped down again and we were in motion, the *Arrow* gliding smoothly forward, picking up speed.

"It's got us!" cried Viriat, and cheered.

We all stared. Dour Viriat never, ever cheered. It occurred to me that for the first time since our shipwreck, he might actually believe we could escape Landfall.

"Settle in," I called over the wind's howl. "Viriat, don't forget your provisions." I seated Halleyne back on her bench, sat with her, wrapped my cloak around her. "You did very, very well," I told her. "We could never reach home without you."

She smiled; then her gaze shifted and her expression turned to surprise. I turned to look.

Viriat had undone the string laced through the neck of the last cloth sack he'd hauled aboard, the big one. Zilona's head now protruded through the bag opening and the rest of her was following as she carefully stood. She was red from the heat and closeness inside that bag but looked in good spirits.

Halleyne turned on me. "You've sneaked her aboard! Why?"

"For her treasure. You were right, I couldn't refuse that resource." I didn't have to tell Zilona to bundle up against the wind; Viriat, solicitous, was already handing her a cloak from another sack.

"But why didn't you tell me?" From her expression and tone I could tell she was ready to become furious. "One day married and you're already plotting behind my back. I knew you were a sneak when I married you—"

"It's my finest trait."

"Yes, it is! But you're not allowed to be a sneak without me!"

I gave her my most ingratiating smile. It wouldn't dissuade her, but it always amused her. "Halleyne, heart of my heart, let me tell you what man has told woman since the childhood of the gods: I did it for you."

"Oh, certainly."

"But this once, it's true. What's your new title again?"

"*Thalahai*. Like your Liedan knights. *Thalahai* and special emissary of the Queen of Terosalle."

"Now, if you knew that the woman who stole Queen Lia's jewels was aboard, wouldn't you be guilty of conspiring against the ruler you're serving as special emissary?"

"Well . . ."

"Yes, you would. You'd be a traitor. Now you're not. You can't go back to tell Herself about the theft; we're already set into motion, you're trapped with the knowledge, you can't do anything about it."

Despite herself, she grinned. "None of which will mean anything when Herself realizes her jewels are missing. The next time we see her, she will accuse me of treason."

"But—important!—you will know she is wrong. You can then argue from a position of absolute certainty. That helps."

"Yes, it does." She sighed and settled back against me. "I can't stay mad at you."

"No?"

"I can't afford to. It's too cold."

❖   ❖   ❖

Viriat got Zilona wrapped up in winter garments far more suitable than the lighter dress she was wearing on the beach, and everyone settled in for the first part of the voyage.

I couldn't believe the speed we made. In spite of the crudeness of our boat, the sheer power of the wind moved us with more than the speed of a galloping horse. The roll of the sea tossed us a little, but neither Jerno nor Zilona, our two most nervous stomachs, evidenced any real discomfort.

It was cold, cold, cold. Little fingers of the wind crept through gaps in our garments and tickled us with chill; we fought a constant war to re-arrange cloaks and coats the better to protect us. Spray frequently sheeted over the bow to strike us in the face; we kept our hoods pulled well up, and we all had arranged to have melthue-hide overcloaks for the voyage. Jenina, our one true sailor, had to hop up at intervals to deal with the sail and its lines; as our wind came around from abeam to nearly behind us, she had to adjust the sail, but gave the wind no satisfaction by betraying discomfort. Jerno, Viriat, and I traded turns handling the steering oar at the stern and bailing the water we inevitably took on; we became very chill during these work shifts.

Halleyne occasionally hummed or sang "The Ride to Hanuman's Point" to reinforce whatever faint tie she had to the wind-spirit. Zilona had little to do, but sat with Halleyne to keep her spirits up when I was on the steering oar.

And we made steady progress on a northwest course. Hope, with us ever since this expedition was planned, began to grow that we would reach home again.

"Where shall we live?" I asked Halleyne.

She gave me a curious look. "That depends on what we find, does it not? If Lia's daughter is the snake we think she is, and rules Terosalle as we believe she must, then Lieda would be the better choice. Otherwise, Terosalle is *far* more sophisticated."

Irked, I said, "I meant, what sort of house. Hill or flatland? City or country? A great, rambling tomb of a home or a narrow thing in the heart of the city with balconies on every facing?"

She laughed. "Are we rich?"

"I think so. I'm a judge. In lean times, I can always sell verdicts."

"City, then, near the royal quarter." She made a broad gesture encompassing the sea around us. "I've had enough vistas and natural beauty to last a lifetime."

When night fell, we settled down for rest. I insisted that everyone sleeping tie himself off to a bench with a length of rope; should disaster strike during the night, no one would be thrown from our canoe.

The canoe was long and broad enough for us to sleep in three pairs laid nearly nose to boot, lying beneath the benches on cross-planks that would keep us above the worst of the water we took on. But the sleeping arrangements provided us with some unforeseen confusion.

In the original plan, I was to lie beside Halleyne in the stern, Jenina was to lie alone beside the mast, and Jerno and Viriat were to crowd into the bow, where their greater bulk and the body heat resulting from it would be some defense against the sheeting spray. But Viriat and Zilona had apparently developed a taste for one another's company—whether during the moons on Fishtail Island or just since I'd assigned him to smuggle her aboard I could not say. When it became clear that they wished to pair up for the night hours, Jenina crossly assigned them the bow, where the water's spray would be worst, and herself took amidships with Jerno—him on one side of the mast, her on the other. Though the wind howl kept me from hearing his words, I saw him chuckling over that; Jenina's dislike of him was well-known.

Oh, and what a night that was. I took first watch on the steering oar. The moon, big and silvery and bright, made the whitecaps on the waves look like floating chunks of ice. I felt as though I were a ghost-steersman forever sailing alone across a sea of ice. But Jenina frequently ruined the illusion by rising to adjust tension on the lines and make sure they were not fraying; many of our lines were made by us from melthue hide strips, not by professional rope-makers, so it was important to keep an eye on them.

When I felt it was time for my shift to end, I prodded Jerno awake and lay again beside Halleyne. She was shivering, half-frozen, her melthue cloak soaked through in places from water above and below; I did as best I could to warm her.

But sleep was nearly impossible. The cold kept me from getting more than a few minutes at a time. Perhaps this was instinct for survival; I did dread falling asleep in that icy wind and never waking up.

By dawn we were all haggard and exhausted.

Not even Jenina could pretend to be immune to the cold; she huddled shivering on her bench whenever she was not tending to our sail. Still, Viriat and Zilona looked pleased with themselves, and we were still making speedy progress toward our homes.

This was the start of the longest and most miserable day of my life. Throughout it we all shook with cold, the deadly monotony of the wind robbing us of life-sustaining heat. We were too chilled to shout over the wind, and so each spoke only to the one beside him—a pleasure for me, though Halleyne and I could not keep our teeth from chattering.

We had a lamp, one of the surviving lamps from the *Wave-Breaker*. Though we'd brought it to signal a ship in case we ran across one, we kept it lit all this day, burning our precious supply of lamp oil, in order that we might pass it from one to another and occasionally warm our hands.

It became harder to stand, with cold-stiffened muscles protesting whenever we did. Another day or two of this, I thought, and we would arrive home dead, a frozen log crewed by men and women made of ice.

Late that night, something other than wind hit us.

I was asleep, in the midst of a fitful doze that, because of my state of exhaustion, had actually gone on more than a few minutes, when I heard Viriat's cry, "Land ho, land ho, stop blowing you bastard, rig for collision—"

I sat up and we collided.

The first blow knocked the bow toward the

skies. In the moonlight I saw Zilona thrown into the air, then yanked short by the tether that attached her to her bench. I heard the grind of a stone or reef scraping along our keel and then it was beneath my own rear, kicking me as hard as any mule through the wood of the canoe. I kept my grip on Halleyne and felt her rise a foot above the planks we sat upon.

Then we came down again; I slammed down onto the planking harder than the blow that sent me up, felt myself slide forward toward the mast, only to be caught up by the rope tied off to my waist. I could feel the canoe skidding, shuddering, across some hard surface, with cracking and snapping all around me; and then the bow hit something too big to move, and we came to a halt.

Even under the howl of the wind, I heard the ominous crack of the mast snapping. It fell forward, toward Zilona, who shrieked and curled into a small ball; but the wind still billowed out the sail and carried the broken mast over the starboard side. It hit something that sounded like stone, and finally everything but the wind was truly still.

"Are you hurt?" I asked my wife.

". . . breathe . . ." she said, a gasp, and I saw that she, like me, had been drawn to the limits of the rope that tied her to the bench. The loop of rope had tightened around her waist and was cutting off her air. I drew out my knife and sliced the rope; she gasped again and drew in a deep breath.

Just forward of the broken remnants of mast, King Jerno stood up. He shouted over the wind, "Is everyone well?"

Zilona waved to show she was not badly hurt. Jenina, near the king, rose, ignoring the king's proffered hand of assistance. I looked back at Viriat; he was folded around the very bench Halleyne and I had been sleeping under, having slid into it from his steersman's perch, and obviously had no breath with which to respond. But he waved to show he was conscious.

"Not too bad, I think," I called forward.

Jenina called, "Where in the hells are we?"

We were on a stony shelf of land decorated with boulders and smaller rocks. It abutted against a hillside sloping sharply upward. Back toward the water lay wreckage shredded from our canoe: The entire outrigging had broken free and lay behind us, and whole chunks of wood had scraped free on boulders in our path.

This place looked like nothing so much as the stony shore of Hopeless Island.

My stomach sank. With the innate perversity of spirits, our wind had led us in a cold, deadly circle and run us aground on the very set of islands we had been fleeing. All strength went out of my legs and I knelt onto the ruined canoe bottom.

Then I recognized the stony hillside before us. Far above, a promontory centrally situated on an otherwise blank oval of rock jutted out like a nose. It was a blank "face" I'd seen many times during the Terosai-Liedan negotiations that took place off—

"Hanuman's Point!" I cried, and rose. "Look there, it's Maramal's Face. We've returned to the Point!"

The others looked, then stared around them,

trying to resolve this moonlit vista into the bleak distant shore they'd seen so many moons ago. One by one, their expressions turned to happy ones, and we let loose a ragged cheer of victory.

Abruptly the tempo of the wind changed. I saw Halleyne's hair pulled free of her hood and whipped about her face. She looked up, left and right, as if tracking the movements of some flying insect, and said, "I understand."

And then the wind was gone.

We looked to her. "What did it say?" I asked.

"Something like, 'Remember my cave.'" She shrugged, amused, and primly sat on the remnants of the nearest bench.

By my recollection, from Maramal's Face it was only part of a day's walk to the nearest fishing village, Seasmith. This would be to the north, into Liedan-controlled territory, which was fine with me.

For now, we arranged to sleep. We found a flat portion of the stone shore as far from the water as we could manage, sheltered by a plate of stone that had buckled up in some distant past, and laid out our travel provisions there—the softest of the pouches for cushions and pillows.

With our wind gone, the night was merely cool, and we collapsed into a sleep we richly deserved.

Midmorning found us in Seasmith, and an odder bunch of visitors its inhabitants had doubtless never seen. We walked in wearing our wool and melthue garments, our stores in bags over our shoulders, our faces—in the case of the men—little less shaggy than our garments. The villagers not already plying their trades on fishing boats gave us odd looks indeed.

While Jerno kept his face hidden under his hood, I spoke to the village headsman, who would have been a harbormaster in a larger town. "Can we hire a boat to carry us to Salgestis?" That city, set in a deep bay, was not far from the great highway leading straight to the capital, Bekalli.

The village headsman, whose beard was like gray wire, nodded but said, "Perhaps. You've papers?"

We looked at one another. "No papers," I said. Since when did one need papers to travel within Lieda's borders?

"No papers, only as far as the border," he said. "Belport."

Belport I knew as well. Four or five days' hard riding south of Salgestis, it was a small seaport situated where the great east-west Knights' Road met the eastern sea.

"Belport it is, then," I told him, keeping my voice confident. "We'll get papers there." Then I dropped my tone to a more confidential one. "Headsman, perhaps you'll help me not to look like an idiot. Moons ago, my brothers and I went up into the mountains to hunt, and to purchase brides among the mountain clans, as our father did before us." My gesture took in the others, and the headsman nodded; bride-buying was an old tradition among the common folk of the border territories, and Viriat and Jerno were, like me, large and bulky men; by shape we could be brothers. And Halleyne, bless her, took on an expression of stoic acceptance, the very appearance of a purchased bride resigned to her fate. "But when we were last through here, this was Liedan territory."

The old man nodded. "No longer. Kingdom of

Bontiniard now." He shrugged. "Taxes the same, and Lieda and Terosai stop fighting over us. Not much has changed. You from Salgestis?"

I nodded.

"You won't have much trouble getting home. Talk to the port authority in Belport. If they don't know your people there, they'll send a message on a boat to Salgestis. A few days, you'll get your permissions."

"Thank you."

He turned to look out to sea. "You can't see it now. Small Carna's sloop. Fast, for all he's not catching much with it. Go down that lane—" he pointed back into the village "—until you see a good stout house with green-and-yellow trim on the shutters. That's Carna's. His wife Naifa will be home. You can dicker with her for passage and leave tomorrow."

"Thanks again." I pressed a coin into his hands, a precious silver penny that I'd carried in my pouch from the day of our shipwreck to this day, and left with my allies.

"Kingdom of *what*?" asked Jenina. Her voice was part whisper, part hiss.

"Bontiniard," I said. "Bontine's Land, in the mountain dialect. That means Sheroit dar Bontine is king here." I too felt like spitting.

Sheroit dar Bontine, master negotiator of the age and a member of the conspiracy designed to rid Lieda and Terosalle of their rightful rulers. Obviously, his reward for treachery had been rule of some of the land the two nations had long held in dispute. I wondered what had happened to his companion, young Teuper, whom I had stabbed during their hasty departure.

We would have to stay out of sight of Bontiniard's ruler here and as far as Belport. No sooner than Salgestis could we begin to think about organizing the rescue expedition.

Only when Halleyne's hand found mine did I realize that I was shaking with anger. I squeezed her hand in return.

"Halleyne, my wife?"

"Yes?"

"Will you still love me if I murder Sheroit dar Bontine?"

"Well, I would prefer it if you ruined him first."

I snorted and relaxed. It was a fine thing to have a wife so understanding. We set out to find Carna's house.

Chapter Four

Carna's wife Naifa was like a fine country apple.
She was big and round, red of complexion, sweet
but a little tart of manner. And Carna's finely-
crafted house was her landbound ship, or so she
ran it, with her children and nieces and nephews
too young to be fishermen acting as her crew.
They fetched us water from the well and cleaned
the dust from our cloaks and boots while we
dickered with Naifa for the services of Carna's
boat.

She was a sharp bargainer, stressing the skills
and services of the boat's crew in making us
comfortable—skills attested to by the attentions
of the children around us—and wringing from us
every penny we would be willing to pay in a village
with other boats to hire.

When all was done and a price agreed upon,
I held up two good-sized gold coins. They had,
until earlier that day, been part of a garish
headdress of Queen Lia's, formed of many Liedan
coins fused to links of a chain. They were worth
far more than the passage we had just booked.
"If I remember," I told her, "this village of
Seasmith is so called because it has many smiths

making iron fittings. Boats put in to buy them for repairs after long voyages, carts put in for repairs when traveling between the two nations."

"Four nations," she corrected me. "But yes, you remember aright." She couldn't take her gaze from the coins.

"Do your smiths make weapons and armor as well?"

"Some, yes."

"Then I wish to engage you to purchase some things for me. Three good swords, if that many are now ready or can be made ready by the time we leave tomorrow, and a good war axe. Length and type, we'll take what we can get. Sheathes for the swords. One good crossbow, twenty-four quarrels, and a quiver. Traveling clothes, two changes for each of us. And if you can find us all this, of whatever money you don't spend on those purchases, minus what we've bargained for already, half comes back to me and half you keep."

She smiled, dimpling. "My house is yours while I am about my errands."

And so it was. She brought in another cousin, a good-sized boy named Palmin, to watch over the little ones and see to our needs while she ran amok in the village making our purchases. Palmin showed a natural interest in our "adventures in the mountains," but we put him off with a few quick-crafted lies and asked him about the changes that had taken place in Feyndala since our departure last autumn.

"I will tell you what the messengers and minstrels tell us," he said. "With Their Majesties sunk by the great autumn storm—I got to tell a royal investigator about that, for I saw it all—

Lieda and the filthy Terosai naturally went back to war."

"Naturally," I said, nodding. From the corner of my eye I saw King Jerno suppress a wry smile.

"Queen Elowar led us in war—Lieda, I mean, when Seasmith still belonged to Lieda—and the Terosai noble council led them, so naturally we thrashed them. But it cost many lives and everyone was tired of it. And that is when Princess Thaliara reappeared."

I tried to look incredulous. "I thought she was long dead."

"Yes! But she wasn't. For years she and the Liedan hero Captain Buyan were prisoners among the Red Lances Mountain Clan." He looked askance at the women. "Are your brides from the Red Lances?"

I saw Jenina bristle. She did not much care for playing the bought-like-livestock bride of Jerno. But her irritation made her role all that much more believable. "No," I said, "they are from the Fiery Tongues Clan."

"Oh. Well, a great mountain king named Jehan of the Black Rock Clan attacked the Red Lances and crushed them, and freed Captain Buyan and Princess Thaliara. They say that she is still as young and beautiful as when she was taken."

"How nice for her. But how did that end the war?"

"Well, Thaliara, who must be much wiser than all the other Terosai, went home and put down those who wanted her mother's throne. She took it herself and made offers of truce to Elowar. War ended for a while and the queens tried to make a peace that would last.

"And then the strange thing happened." The boy looked ingenuous and waited. I gave him a cross look and he continued, "The Feyndalan League."

"And what is that?"

"The mountain clan-lord, Jehan, proclaimed that he could make lasting peace between the kingdoms. Many messengers were sent to him. Ambassadors went from both nations to the citadel he is building high in the mountains. And when all was done, Queen Elowar and Queen Thaliara gave him the mountain lands and the disputed territories."

An explosion of noise from Jerno: "*All* of them?"

The boy jumped. "Yes, my lord. They wrote treaties and exchanged gifts and when all was done, the mountains were the nation of Hiaraniard. The three nations made a pact of friendship. The Feyndalan League. They protect one another. When they disagree, the three rulers cast votes, and King Jehan's is the biggest vote."

Jerno looked among us as though he feared he was again losing his mind. "This is . . . not like the nobles. Of either nation."

The boy shrugged. "All nobles are mad. So my father says."

I interrupted. "What of Bontiniard?"

"Well, we were first made part of Hiaraniard. But not so long ago, Sheroit dar Bontine returned. You've heard of him?"

"Oh, yes," I said.

"He was on the treaty boats that were lost. He and a lad were washed up on a little island and wintered there. They built a raft and returned home. And do you know who the lad was?"

"No," I said, lying through gritting teeth.

"Prince Teuper. King Jehan's son and heir. King Jehan was so grateful for dar Bontine trying to end the war, and for saving his son, that he just gave him this end of Hiaraniard to rule for his own." The boy beamed. "It is good, you know? Dar Bontine was a commoner when he was a boy, that's what they say. Now he is a king. And all he had to do was guide noblemen toward agreement and wash up on the right beach."

"May he do so again. It is good of you to keep such open ears and eyes," I told the boy. "I will commend you to your aunt."

He smiled. And when he was next off on an errand, I talked in hushed tones with the others.

Jerno fumed. "Elowar would never give up all the Liedan mountain territories just to end the war."

"Are you sure?" Halleyne asked. "The war cost her three sons, too. She may have been more weary of it than you."

"I can well imagine her giving up the disputed territories," the king said. "But the undisputed lands? To make up a new kingdom for this Jehan? No. That is not Elowar. Something else is at work here." He turned to me. "You mentioned the name Jehan once before. Long ago."

"Teuper's father, as the boy said, a foreign adventurer. He directed the conspiracy to drown us. Now we see the further steps of his plans."

"I'll see to it that he steps no more." The king held his hands before him and closed them around an imaginary throat.

"Remember," said Jenina, "our first goal is the rescue expedition. What are our options now?"

I ticked items off on my fingers. "Well, first,

from what I learned from Teuper moons ago, and from what we can reason now, it is certain that Thaliara and Buyan betrayed their respective royal parents and allowed this war to rage while they conspired with Jehan. Thaliara will not be willing to let Lia return to resume her throne. So we should not try to launch our rescue from Terosalle. If rumor reached the new queen we would be lost."

"Bontiniard is also not an option," Zilona said quietly.

"Correct. For the same reasons. Second, Queen Elowar has made political decisions King Jerno doesn't understand. She may have been far more frantic to end the war than we realized—but the king, who knows her best, says this is unlikely. Or perhaps Jehan and the others have some hold on her, a hold great enough to make her give up valuable territories but not great enough to make her give up her throne. So we have to presume that our enemies are strong in Lieda, too."

Viriat stirred. "What does that leave us?"

"We have to fulfill the promise we made. Get everyone off Landfall before Snake-Mother awakens. I think we must do so from Lieda— I've thought so all along, which is why I booked us passage to the Liedan border—and must arrange our expedition from there. Which means Salgestis, the nearest Liedan port with ships for hire large enough to take the survivors off Fishtail."

We spent the night in relative comfort on Carna's porch, stuffed full of Naifa's good bread and stew, the best meal any of us had had in moons. In the morning we boarded Naifa's little clipper, six very changed men and women.

Packed were the garments we had worn from Landfall. In their place we wore good Liedan clothes of linen and wool. Viriat and I shaved, for Naifa had bought us a good razor without asking, as it was clear to her that we had not shaved during our mountain expedition. But Jerno kept his beard, the better to disguise his face, made famous by paintings and the stamping of coins.

Of the weapons I ordered, one of the broadswords went to Jerno, the other to Viriat. I took the shortsword, a weapon easier to conceal and more in line with the way I preferred to fight— up close, aiming for the guts—on the rare occasions I was forced to do so. Once we parted company with Carna, Jenina would get the axe; she'd said once that she wished to be armed, but had no training with blades, so I got her a weapon more like the sorts of tools she was used to from ship's duties. And the crossbow went to Viriat; he was the trained bodyguard, best to give him all the weapons he could manage.

So we left Seasmith as good, common Liedan men with resigned mountain brides, and neither Carna nor his crew expressed any suspicion of our story.

Two days later we were in Belport, a small, smelly seaside city, now the northernmost point of the hatefully-named nation of Bontiniard. We said farewell to Carna, paying him the remainder of his fee, and headed straight to the marketplace. There, I changed another of Queen Lia's gold coins for a handful of silver and copper Liedan (and new Hiaraniard) coins, and sought out a jeweler's.

"To trade in more of Herself's treasure?" the king asked.

"No, to bypass guards and authorities and get into Lieda."

He scowled. "How will a jeweler do that?"

"Think about it. What is Belport's claim to fame in trade?"

"Well, jewelry."

"Correct. It takes pearls brought in from merchant boats, gold and precious stones brought down from the mountains, and makes them into jewelry, which it then sends off to other markets."

"So?"

"But now Belport is part of Bontiniard, with a border that is regulated."

"Kin, I do not like guessing games. You are making me very angry." He sounded thoughtful rather than angry.

Halleyne spoke up. "What my less than informative husband is trying to tell you is this. Belport now has a border between it and its favored customers in Lieda. In addition to making fine citizens such as ourselves resort to papers of transit, a border means new taxes and tariffs, which honest craftsmen who are unused to having them will not wish to pay."

"Ah. You're saying that they will be smuggling some of their wares into Lieda."

"Correct," I said. "And if they know how to get their own people past border checkpoints, they are also likely to sell us the information on how to do so."

I stopped outside a streetcorner business; the painted sign above the door said "Trieme's Goldwrights, Makers of the Crown of King Lavvan."

"My grandfather," said the king, and touched his own brow where a crown once rested.

"What's good enough for him is probably good enough for us," I told him.

I need not go into too much detail on how we got out of Belport. Trieme's great-grandson Trieme had a nephew also named Trieme, and for a stout fee he led us out of Belport just before the gates closed at twilight; we kept a cold camp in the woods not far from the town, and in the dawn light followed an old hunter's trail through the woods until we were miles past the Liedan border. Then it was a simple matter to turn south again to the unpaved Knights' Road that ranged from sea to sea across the breadth of Lieda. There, we persuaded a farmer returning from a trip to the seaside city to carry us to Crossroads, the trade town that lay where Knights' Road met the Royal Highway; we had the itchy pleasure of riding in the back of a mostly-empty hay wagon.

On the first night, as we camped near the roadway, in the small hours before dawn, I heard Halleyne's name being called. She didn't stir, but I did, rolling sleepily to look up.

Shallia stood over my lady-love, quietly calling her name, imploring her to awaken.

It was odd that Shallia stood there, as we'd left her back on Fishtail Island less than a week before, but that was not the oddest thing. Stranger still was the fact that, though Shallia cast her shadow on the two of us, when she moved I could see the stars and moon through her.

I swore and said, "Shallia?" But she did not react. She reached as though to take Halleyne's shoulder, but could not seem quite to reach it.

My outburst awoke Viriat and the farmer who was conveying us toward Crossroads. The latter, a plain fellow, simple of speech, looked at the woman he could see through, jumped up, and ran away from our fire as fast as his legs would carry him.

I shook Halleyne awake. When she saw Shallia's specter she sat up against me and called her friend's name.

I saw relief on Shallia's face. She spoke, but the pitch of her voice was so low I could hear only occasional words: ". . . find you . . . practice this . . . has been a murder . . . among us . . . pray you dispatch . . ."

Then, between one moment and the next, she was gone. Everyone in camp was now sitting up, rubbing sleep-bleary eyes, staring at us.

"What in the hells was that?" This was Jerno. "Was that the girl's ghost-spirit? Is she dead?"

Halleyne shook her head, her expression full of wonder. "Her spirit, yes, but not a ghost. She lives. I didn't understand all she was saying. This is something she has practiced since we left, trying to find me, to send me her thoughts as we both slept. She said she will try again . . ."

"What was that about a murder?" I asked.

"There has been one. She said there is a madman among them. She begs for us to send the rescue ship. I understood little more than that. Maybe I can try to reach out for her instead; perhaps my spirit-magic can hook her and reel her in so her voice will be louder next time."

Jerno flopped back over onto his blanket. "I had hoped," he said, "that when we returned home things would be a bit more normal."

The farmer did not return to us the next morning. We took his wagon and oxen and continued on toward Crossroads. In the three days more it took us to reach the city, Shallia did not manifest herself to Halleyne again, nor for some time after that.

In Crossroads, we turned over the oxen and wagon to the farmer's wife and explained that he'd be along soon. When we were through with that errand, I said, "Now, Majesty, you can speak to the city authorities and arrange transportation home . . . if you choose."

"If I choose. You mean, if I am willing to declare myself now and ride into Bekalli with the whole world knowing of my coming."

"Yes."

He shook his head. "Until I know what prompted Elowar to give up such valuable territories, until I know what influences lie close to her, I think I will keep this beard. Why don't you arrange us more anonymous transportation and find out what we can expect in Salgestis."

Viriat, after spending some time talking with traders in a tavern, convinced me that Salgestis would do us no good.

"The winter was fair in Lieda, foul in Terosalle," he said. "The Liedan trader fleets grouped up in Salgestis until the winter broke a few weeks ago, then sailed. You'll find no ship larger than Carna's there for weeks to come."

"Except for naval vessels," Jerno said. "Did you find out who the naval commander is at Salgestis?"

"Yes. Admiral Ariens Desero."

"*Admiral* Desero? He was captain last I knew. And he loathes me from behind his smiling face." Jerno sighed. "Our best chance is Bekalli. There will be ships for hire there—at worst, even if I can find no naval captain loyal to me, there will always be one merchant captain or another with his ship impounded until he can pay old debts."

"Bekalli it is, then," I said.

Halleyne helped us preserve our anonymity. She used makeup she'd purchased in Belport to change all our features, giving me and Zilona distracting moles, shadowing Viriat's nose to make it seem as though it had been once broken and then ill-set, coloring Jenina's hair to a midnight black and requiring her to wear it loose rather than in a telltale sailor's braid.

Then we hired a coach that regularly made the two-week journey back to the capital of Bekalli and were finally, finally on the way home.

On our long journey, we saw signs of peace everywhere. The caravans of goods sent to supply our ships and armies were nowhere to be seen, replaced by caravans of trade goods. Marching armies did not clog the roads. In the towns and cities, royal hospitals servicing the military were not filled to the rafters with injured fighting-men and women. But with all these cheerful signs, King Jerno became increasingly glum.

Once, the third day out, as we were passing

the port of Salgestis, I asked him why he was so gloomy. He answered me, "I wonder if the war will resume when I take the throne again. I would prevent that if I could."

Jenina, ever helpful, asked, "And if you learn that taking the throne means the war will start again, no matter what you do?"

"Then I do not know," he said.

Zilona said, "You would take the throne anyway, Majesty. Be comforted; no ruler would willingly abandon his throne. You have little choice in the matter."

In the many towns where we spent our nights, we could afford to take rooms at good inns—the sort of inns that kept a hedge-mage on staff to cast the spells that keep lice, bedbugs, and ticks at bay. With an abundance of money at our disposal, we took four rooms each time, with Halleyne and I in one, Viriat and Zilona, increasingly attached, in another, and Jerno and Jenina each having one.

Three weeks after departing Fishtail Island, we clattered into Bekalli, wearing good new clothes and carrying good new weapons, well-furnished with gold and plans, ready to shake up the rulers of all Feyndala.

And Bekalli was the place from which to launch such an effort. You who have never seen the great city would do well to learn of it. Imagine it in your mind's eye:

On the ragged north coast of Feyndala, a deep bay cuts almost due south, two days' fast sailing deep, one day's wide. Where the coast turns from eastward to northward, there lies Bekalli, a great port town, its hardy wooden docks and stone piers jutting out into the water like the teeth of a curved comb, numberless boats tied off to them. The city sprawls inland along flat, rich soil thickly dotted with trees.

The old city, the portions closest to the harbor, has cobblestone streets and tight-packed brick homes, many of them a narrow two-stories stacked side by side, some of them two and three sagging centuries in age. It is there that my family's home is to be found, a flaking edifice outside with good beams and level floors inside. A great wall of dressed stone surrounds the old city, with three gates allowing traffic into the middle city.

The middle city, radiating outward from the old city in all directions, has some streets of cobblestone and some of brick, some areas of wealthy homes and some commoner's warrens, and on the only hill in the region the separately-walled citadel of the king. The middle city, too, is walled, protected by a stout curtain of dressed stone designed in the likeness of the old city's wall but two centuries younger. Gates in this wall allow egress to the new city.

The new city sprawls out from the middle. It has been many decades since any invader brought land forces as far north as Bekalli; for this reason, long ago, daring citizens bought land and built homes outside what are now the middle city walls. Though they may not build within a hundred paces of the walls, that broad margin has become home to the day-market, where numberless tents and stands are set up during the daylight hours but must be struck by night. It is the most thriving portion of the city. A wall is planned for it, too, and has been for many years, with no construction yet having taken place.

Old, middle, and new, home to more than three hundred thousand people, Bekalli offered all the variety and opportunity one could ever ask for, and it was my home. When we were on the long stretch of road leading to it, and I finally saw the dark bump that was the royal citadel, my heart leapt.

Hours later, as twilight was threatening to fall, we crossed the ditch that marked the new city's borders, the ditch that would someday be the boundaries of the new curtain wall, and were among the ill-built wooden homes of the new city's poorer residents. I cheered at seeing familiar buildings until Halleyne hushed me. Not long after, the coachman let us off at the Bekalli station of his stage business, a short walk from my house.

My house. My family's house, rather; it had been many years since I lived there, many moons since I visited. When my father was younger and recently come to generalship, as his star was ascending, he had bought not just one of the old city's town homes, but four all in a row, constituting a whole block of dilapidated housing. He'd left the exterior much as it had always looked but spent the rewards King Jerno had lavished upon him in refurbishing the interior, opening doorways between what had once been separate dwellings, replacing floors and ceilings, bringing in fine naval woodworkers to make a sumptuous interior in teak and other rich woods.

Today, as the six of us, fugitives all, stood before my family's house, it was little changed. The exterior was all courses of bricks, no longer laid in straight lines because of sagging ground, with many windows bricked over, others covered with heavy shutters. A weathered, intimidating, scowling visage, much like that of my father, I decided.

I hammered with the door-knocker.

A long wait; Old Tyasan, the door-servant, must be sleeping, I thought.

Finally, I heard the thumping and pounding of the door being unbarred, and it creaked in protest as it was pulled open.

There stood my father. I was used to him seeming small, for I had grown taller than he years ago; I was used to him seeming old, for when the war took his eldest son he suddenly gained many years and white-gray hairs. But I was not used to seeing him lifeless; there was no spark in his eyes, no strength in his arm as he held a lamp aloft, no real curiosity in his voice as he asked, "Who comes?"

I threw back my hood. "Father, it's Kin. May we come in?"

For a moment, confusion flickered in his eye. Then he strode forward and embraced me for the first time since I was a young man leaving home for service in the king's citadel.

Once we were inside, confusion reigned. Father barred the door behind us and shooed us into the main hall, the place where, during my childhood, leaping fires were built and powerful men gathered to boast of military and romantic accomplishment; all the while, Father shouted up the stairs, "Ansha, come down, come down, come down!"

In moments my mother, grayer and slighter than I remembered her, was at the door to the main hall, and seeing me she shrieked and flew to me like a bird. Dyack and his wife Ballia, two of the family servants, came to investigate the noise and set to laying in a fire and bringing out food for us. Words swirled about us like leaves in the wind, so many that it was hard to associate them with those who spoke them: "Kin, how did you—" "—gone all these moons, why did you not—" "—gods have sent you—" "—prepare yourself for news that is not so happy—"

I held up my hands to get their attention. "I'll tell you every part of the story soon enough. First, I must say this: You must not tell anyone, *anyone*, that I am home. Dyack, Ballia, you either. Gossip could be fatal for me." I waited until I caught all their eyes and knew they understood. "Second, I must introduce my traveling companions." I gestured at the largest one among us. "Him, of course, you already know. Allow me to present His Majesty, Jerno Byriver, king by the authority of the gods over Lieda, but not, I understand, over some mountain provinces and previously disputed territories."

The king obliged me by flipping back his hood at the moment I spoke his name and beaming at my father.

The servants knelt. Father and Mother did not. One of the few traits of Jerno's I'd found admirable was his willingness to dispense with customs of kingly honor and power in all but the most official of circumstances. But Father saluted and Mother gave him an appropriate curtsy, both of them with shock upon their faces.

Jerno stepped forward to take Father's hand. "General Underbridge. I regret to inform you that I've granted your worthless son the rank of Judge of Lieda, meaning his rank exceeds yours and you must find some new way to keep him in line."

My parents looked at me disbelievingly. I shrugged and continued before they could speak. "Next, the former Halleyne dar Dero, one-time handmaiden and scribe for the queen of Terosalle, now a *thalahai* of that court—and now my wife and your daughter, Halleyne Underbridge."

That was the end of the introductions. Mother fainted, and Father, catching her and lowering her to the bench of the nearest table, looked as though he might follow her into oblivion.

Once restoratives were applied—a stinking aromatic to rouse Mother, and a goblet half-filled with hard liquor to calm Father—I told them the whole story. I dared not risk my mother's nerves again; I told the tale in as soothing a manner as I could. Both the king and Halleyne interrupted at times to play up my part in the events that had transpired, disrupting what I considered to be a skillful narrative flow . . . but one cannot tell one's king or a wife like Halleyne to take a seat and be quiet.

The servants fed us during my story; when it was done, I was the only one who had had little to eat, so I began an assault on the plate before me.

Mother, her tone subdued, said to Halleyne, "I hope you will forgive me my startlement. I'd long waited for Kin to wed. It just startled me that you were, you were—"

"Terosai," Halleyne said. Her tone was conversational; her Liedan was perfect.

"Halleyne!"

Mother looked regretful. "But it's true, Kin. Your brother Tan died at Terosai hands. So did your brother Tesker—"

I felt as though someone had punched out my wind. "Tesker dead?"

She nodded slowly, mournfully. "When war began again he made ensign. But his ship went down . . ." She swallowed.

My head swam. Young Tesker, four years my junior. He would not even have been one-and-twenty when he died. A stone formed in my throat and no amount of swallowing would dislodge it. I felt Halleyne's hand seek mine and I clutched at it as though it would save me from drowning.

Mother turned back to Halleyne. "So it was a surprise," she continued. "But I know there are fine Terosai out there; my husband has fought them. I know there are foul Liedans; my husband has executed them. And Kin is no fool. I know he has chosen well. I welcome you to my family, Halleyne. I am happy you carry our name."

My wife merely said, "Thank you." But her smile was so bright that it did much to banish the melancholy I felt.

King Jerno turned to my father. "Lay it out for me, General Underbridge, like little units on a map. What do I face when I undertake to regain my throne?"

Father considered. "By declaration of your queen, you are dead."

"Easily dealt with. I must merely appear before the Council of Judges and force them to recognize me. Which they will. My own cousin is chief judge—does he still live?"

Father nodded and continued. "When decisions

you have made while you were absent conflict with Queen Elowar's, the queen's carry more weight . . . and yours are not truly in effect until the council recognizes that you still live."

"So my divorce from Elowar does not take effect until then."

"Yes. If you wish to bring that up. You might find it more helpful to forget about it."

The king regarded him steadily. "It's true that I set her aside for less than admirable reasons. In my right mind, I would not have done such a thing. Though I still must sire an heir, doubtless on a royal mistress."

Father waved that thought away. Personal matters of the marriage between Jerno and Elowar made him uncomfortable. "More to the point, the decisions she has made . . . giving up the mountain provinces and the disputed territories, joining the Feyndalan League . . . are not something you can easily set aside. War would result."

Jerno's tone became a growl. "What is behind that bit of madness?"

"I don't know. But Elowar signed the treaty, and your most powerful nobles made it clear they supported her." Father looked apologetic. "I am not in her confidence as I was in yours, Majesty. I have scarce seen her since your throne was taken from the citadel's great hall. I will say she seems sure of vision and filled with vigor."

"Scarcely the attitude of a grieving widow," Jerno said.

We, on the other hand, were not filled with vigor, and it was not long afterward that Mother had the servants make ready our rooms. The remaining servants, I should say; the army was being reduced in force, Father was no longer active, and to hoard his pension he had dismissed many members of the staff and closed off portions of the house.

Halleyne and I had my old room, closed for many years. Jerno was given my brother Tan's, closed for even longer, and Viriat had Young Tesker's beside it. Zilona had my sister Fara's, Fara my sole surviving sibling, for all she lived weeks' travel to the south, in the city of Samaithe; yet I thought, deep in the night, I heard the creak of light footsteps leading from that room to Viriat's. And Jenina had to make due in the old butler's room; scarcely a burden, for he'd had a chamber bigger than mine.

So many strangers in rooms I'd known since youth. It was unsettling. But we were back in Bekalli, poised to make arrangements to rescue the other castaways and reseat Jerno on his throne; I lay with my wife in the house that might again be mine some day, and knew that my parents, for all their trepidation, had begun to accept her.

For that night only, things were good.

Chapter Five

A heavy blow against my door awoke me.

I knew at once what had happened. Some sharp-eyed guard had seen us enter Bekalli, had recognized the king, had informed the palace. Now guards filled the halls of my family's home, ready to take us to prison or cut us down trying. I was half out of bed, sword in hand, before I realized that there was no shouting going on, no clash of weapons, no demand for admission.

I looked at Halleyne, who was tousled and blinking, rousing from sleep. I could see the window shutters were limned by daylight—it must be midmorning at the earliest. "Who goes?" I asked.

"Viriat." His voice was a croak.

I set the sword down, threw on a robe, and opened the door. Viriat must have been leaning against it; he staggered in, half-dressed, his face tragic. He thrust a piece of paper at me.

It read,

> *Dearest Viriat:*
> *It is not just soldiers and heroes who "must do what must be done." Sometimes it is ladies-*

in-waiting, though it cost us everything. Though it cost me you.

I hope you will find some way to forgive me. If you can, come to me on that day, and we will be not apart. If you decide you never can, come to me on that day and strike me down, for I will not live knowing you loathe me.

I remain your Zilona, twice traitress.

"Oh, gods," I said.

"What is it?" asked Halleyne.

"I'm not sure. Nothing good." I flipped the paper to her and retrieved my trousers.

"There's another one by the door," she said, and scanned the note in her hand.

She was right; another note lay before the door, as if slid beneath it. I took it up.

It read,

To my dear sister in service, Halleyne dar Dero, now Halleyne Underbridge—and what a funny name that is—this letter is addressed.

Halleyne, I hope you will forgive me. You can only do so if you know that what I do today is not from self-interest.

In your desire to return home, you have forgotten something very important. Queen Lia is the lowest sort of bitch-dog, biting to death those who serve her, and for her to resume the throne of Terosalle would be the cruelest sort of punishment for all our people and all our families.

In like manner, King Jerno, a madman by his own confession, cannot be allowed to resume his royal rank and titles. It would be wrong.

For this reason, I have parted company with you. I go now to the Liedan palace, bearing proof of Jerno's survival and Herself's, which I will present to the Liedan queen Elowar. I will tell her the story of our exile on Landfall, the way he set her aside and planned to raise another queen over her, that she might take steps to capture and punish her former husband. When I have done here, I will travel back to Terosalle, where I will tell the same things to Queen Thaliara.

In the natural course of things, it will be many hours, if not days, even with the proofs I offer, before I am conducted to the queen's presence. Use this time to part ways with Jerno. Drive him forth from this place; I will not mention House Underbridge when I tell the tale. With the treasures in your position, you can still arrange for the rescue of those remaining on Fishtail Island.

It is my dearest wish that you will understand why I have done this and forgive me from your heart.

With kindest thoughts, I remain your friend, Zilona.

I passed that note as well to my wife. "She certainly asks for a lot of forgiveness. Damn her." I ran for the hall and the stairs. "Mother! When did Zilona leave?"

In minutes we were all awake and some answers were forthcoming. After writing the notes with paper and ink Mother had given her, Zilona had left just after dawn with the cook, Ballia, ostensibly to shop with her in the grocer's market; we had nearly cleared the pantries of food last night. Zilona had made the reasonable argument to Mother that no one in Bekalli knew her, so there was no chance of her accidentally giving away the fact of our return. "Accidentally is the key word," Halleyne said in a hiss. "Doubtless she's slipped away from Ballia and is cooling her heels in the royal waiting-hall even now. Damn, damn, damn." Then she looked around guiltily to see if my parents had heard her mild oaths.

"This is very bad," the king said. "Zilona will poison Elowar so that no words I can spin will cause her to forgive me." He stood with his chin in his hand and looked sorrowful. Then he looked curiously at his hand and headed off for the stairs.

"Viriat," I said, "had you no sign that this was coming?"

"No," he said, helplessness in his face and voice. "Yes, she railed against her queen. Endlessly. Tirelessly. But I'd heard all her ladies-in-waiting do that at one time or another."

King Jerno came thundering down the stairs again. "Curse the girl, she's taken it," he said, waving his hand about. "My ring. My royal seal. She must have stolen into my room while I slept."

Halleyne took a good look at my face. "I must guess this makes the situation worse," she said.

"Much. Our palace is not quite like yours, dear heart. We Liedans can let unwanted visitors cool their heels as long as you Terosai, but we're not quite so mired in protocol as Queen Lia. If a young woman were to come to the palace claiming to have seen the lost king within the last day, and waving his royal seal around as proof—"

"They have only to summon the royal jeweler," Jerno said. "In minutes, he would confirm the ring to be genuine. And minutes later Zilona would be conducted into the presence of the queen. She's probably there already, and the hours of time she thought we'd have are gone."

I turned to the king. "Majesty, I'm going to hire a ship this very day. If I can, we'll be out of Bekalli Harbor before nightfall. If you hurry, you might get to the palace before Zilona does too much damage."

"I'm not going to the palace."

"You surprise me."

He was slow in answering. "I want to address my queen, yes. But I am finding that when I do what I most want, it is often not rational. Witness my marriage to Shallia. If instead I do what I *plan*, things work better. And our plan, to which I swore allegiance, was to effect the rescue of the others before any other concern."

"True. That is well-reasoned of you."

Jenina, hearing the king's words, stood there gaping, the expression on her face indicating that she did not recognize the man who spoke them. I couldn't blame her. Truth be told, I could barely recognize him myself.

"Pack up," I said. "I want us out of here in less time than it takes to cook an egg. Father, Mother, erase any signs that we were here."

Father nodded gruffly; Mother looked resigned. They, and all my companions but the king, hurried off about this business. And I realized, belatedly, that for the first time I'd issued an order to my own parents. Even more miraculously, they were doing what I said instead of beating my ears with a cane.

I helped Halleyne pack up our few belongings. Mother brought us clothes scavenged from the quarters of lost family members and departed servants, that we might have a change of garments . . . and more authentic Liedan clothes to wear today. Then we congregated in the kitchen and, after embraces for my parents, ducked out the back way—a sturdy door that opened into the alley between my parents' home and the block of buildings behind.

Since we reasoned that any city guards out hunting for us would be looking for a band of five, we chose to head separately for the harbor and our missions. For the first part of our day, Jerno and Jenina would take a room at the Ship's Rat, which, despite its name, was a good clean inn favored by ships' officers; it overlooked much of the harbor area. They would send runners to the naval officers loyal to him and arrange confidential meetings. Viriat would be there as well, spending time in the taproom downstairs. Halleyne and I would see about the possibility of hiring a merchantman or other civilian ship large enough to carry our castaways. And should we become truly separated, we planned to look in, dusk and dawn, at the Sea-Goat, a less reputable tavern in the new city, until we were reunited.

Halleyne and I walked the length of the harbor, looking for a ship of the right size bearing telltale signs of financial difficulty. There were a few; over

the years of the war, many merchant companies
had failed, and others were still on the verge of
doing so.

At taverns and the harbormaster's, we made
inquiries about the ships I'd noted, learned about
the disposition of the captains and what they owed,
and crossed from my list a pair of likely prospects
that turned out to have been impounded by the
crown. Of the ones that remained, the *Driftwood*,
an ancient galleon owned and captained by one
Ehan Planker, seemed the best prospect, so it
is there we visited a little after midday.

No one but a guard, a carpenter, and a pair
of sailors repairing ropes were aboard. The
younger sailor was sent to fetch the captain from
his nearby home.

I looked about the ship and liked what I saw.
Despite the fact that debt kept the ship at anchor,
the captain was finding funds somewhere for
repairs, and the good condition of the vessel
suggested that Planker attended small matters as
well as big ones.

From the rail, Halleyne asked, "That's the Ship's
Rat again, isn't it?"

I looked east along the line of wooden piers.
"That's it. In fact, if they have done as they should,
they have a room looking out over the harbor.
They may be looking at you even now."

She waved at the tavern just in case I was
correct. "Oh, this must be your captain."

And indeed it was. Accompanying the returning
sailor was a portly, middle-aged man wearing what
had, twenty years ago, been quite a fine formal
captain's coat and hat; though faded, the garments
were in good condition. He ambled up the

gangplank, received the guard's salute as he came
aboard, and headed straight for us. "My lord—?"

"Fishtail," I said. I saw Halleyne repress a
snicker, and I continued, "And this is Milady
Turtlehead." I ignored her glare.

"I am Captain Planker. The boy said you wished
to speak of engaging my vessel. Would you care
to speak in my cabin? It's a bit cramped there,
but secure. Or perhaps on the poop deck?"

At my nod, he led us aft and up the ladder
to his poop deck. I felt a little better staying under
the sun with a clear view of all the harbor.

"And what sort of expedition are you planning?"

"Sail to a specific spot in uncharted waters.
About a hundred and twenty marches' sailing from
here. Put in at an island and take on cargo to
return to Feyndala."

"Cargo. Uncharted waters." He looked amused.
"It sounds as though you've found a map from
the old days of reaving and pirating. Someone's
long-hidden treasure?"

"Nothing so romantic," Halleyne said. "The
cargo is plants, animals, living things. The island
has many specimens not seen on Feyndala, such
as the long-bearded gulbuk and the dreaded
Gloriana viper. We plan to take them on tour
throughout Lieda. A new show, Fishtail and
Turtlehead's Exotic Entertainments."

"Ah." The captain considered. I could see he
was calculating. "And where, exactly, is this island?"

I told him, "I cannot say until we leave port.
Our competitors have keen ears. It will, however,
be in southern climes, not northern."

"It would be just you accompanying the ship?
Or the two of you?"

"We two, possibly two or three others."

He fell to calculating again.

Halleyne touched my elbow. I looked at her, at her narrowed eyes, and followed her gaze.

A wagon carrying city guardsmen had just pulled to a stop before the Ship's Rat. The uniformed men rushed in a line into the tavern. I felt my stomach sink.

The captain said, "Well, unaccustomed as I am to accepting engagements with so little information before me, I find myself in circumstances that make me more than usually agreeable. But I will need funds up front—"

How like a merchant captain to leap right into the negotiation. I'd hoped merely to find out which ships and captains suited me and get a sense of how much it would cost. But what was happening at the tavern suggested that King Jerno's loyal officers might have just been removed from our list of resources.

"I'm prepared to offer you fifty royal crowns to buy your ship's freedom from the royal tax collectors," I told him. As the last of the soldiers entered the tavern, a tall figure I recognized as Viriat emerged, his crossbow, still wrapped in wool, over his shoulder. He picked up a stone from the street and hurled it against a shuttered window above. "In addition, my quartermaster will work with yours during reprovisioning and will pay for provisions directly." The shutters opened and Jerno leaned out. I saw Viriat calling up to him. One of the two guardsmen who had stayed with the wagon and horses approached Viriat. "Finally, five royal crowns which you may spend to hire crewmen."

"That's scarcely enough to pay for a full crew complement for a mission that may take two or three moons." The captain's tone was quite reasonable.

Viriat turned to the soldier and set down his crossbow. Then he kicked the soldier in the kneecap. The man fell, waving his arms about; Viriat drew his sword and slashed the man's leg. The other soldier ran toward him, drawing his own sword.

"True. And there may be a bonus if my own patron is pleased with your command and your crew's work. But I will not guarantee this. At worst, you'll be out of debt except to your crew, and immediately on return to Lieda can resume your merchant business."

The king disappeared from the tavern window and Jenina appeared there, sliding out, sitting on the windowsill.

A flurry of motion below her; Viriat did something, whirling his cape with his left hand, a motion that baffled the guardsman; Viriat struck and the guardsman fell, redness flowing from his chest or neck.

"True," the captain agreed, grudging. "What's all that?"

"Some sort of brawl at the tavern." Halleyne tried to sound dismissive, but I could hear the tremor of worry in her voice.

Jenina dropped to the cobblestones, quickly stood, and moved aside, looking up. Viriat took the sword of the second guard and ran to the tavern door, placing the weapon through the rings that served the two doors as handles. Jerno squeezed out through the window and perched on the sill as Jenina had; then he glanced over his shoulder back into the room and pushed off in a hurry. He hit far less gracefully than Jenina, but stood with her help.

"It's much calmer than it was before the season's sailing began," the captain said. "Oh, look at the fat one run. He's faster than he looks."

I saw three guardsmen crowd into the window above. One tried to bring a crossbow to bear, but the others were pressed in too tight; he shook them free and aimed, but my allies were already rounding a corner. The three guards pulled back out of sight.

"What I offer you is a fortune to me, Captain, and it's all I have," I said, and that was the truth. "That means we can dicker from now till sunset and I'll still have no more to give you. The same amount means freedom for your ship and resumption of your career. What say you?"

The front doors of the tavern pulled inward but were arrested by the sword before they could open more than a couple of handspans. Someone on the inside grasped the sword through the gap and began sliding it to one side. The guardsman who'd only been slashed in one limb got up on the other leg and began hopping toward the door.

"Done," said the captain.

I turned, saw he was extending his hand, and I took it.

"When do you wish to set sail?" he asked.

"Soon. Tonight or tomorrow, if you can gather a crew and provisions that soon." I took the pouch from my waist and began counting out royal crowns and smaller coins that I'd been trading royal jewels for. "If you wish to save yourself the fee of a first mate, I will supply you with one. Experienced, tough. She will also navigate you to our destination."

"At this point, I will save fees wherever I can." His tone was amused rather than resigned. I concluded that he was more pleased than displeased with our deal.

From the corner of my eye I saw many guardsmen spill out of the Ship's Rat. Some set out after the king and companions on foot; others piled back onto the wagon.

I handed the captain his up-front money. "Good to be working with you, Captain Planker."

Though the day was mostly one of disasters, two things went right. We had successfully commissioned a ship, and at dusk we found Jerno, Jenina, and Viriat at the Sea-Goat Tavern.

Halleyne and I made our way through the ill-smelling mass of lower-class drinkers and diners; I struck one man, a dung collector from the smell of him, who reached for my wife, and he obligingly passed out, doubtless more from what he'd drunk than from my blow. No one took notice of the blow except a man at the next table, who applauded. Then we seated ourselves with our comrades.

"Are you all well?" Halleyne asked. "We saw your flight."

"I twisted my ankle," the king said. "It's better now. But the guards are out in force looking for me. There are notices being posted, claiming that an impostor with the dead king's mien is hiding in the city, fomenting rebellion." He looked half-amused.

"We have a ship," I said, and gave them the details, interrupted only by the arrival of a serving-boy; a minute later, he brought beer and a ploughman's supper for Halleyne and me. "Jenina, you are crucial now; tomorrow at dawn, I want you at the *Driftwood*. Push, lash, curse, do whatever you can to get the boat provisioned, crewed, and out to sea as soon as you can." I gave her most of the coin remaining in my pouch.

She smiled. "At last you've given me something to do that I do well."

Through our meal, Viriat didn't speak. His face had settled into neutral lines, its usual appearance. But his eyes were bleak.

"I took a room for us at the Silver Bit," Jenina said.

I restrained a groan. The inn she named was once a barn. The lower floor was still a stable, the upper floor having been built up into rooms for hire. The smell of horse manure floated up through gaps in the flooring. Not an enjoyable place. But I recalled that some of the rooms were accessible by exterior stairs; doubtless she'd obtained us quarters there for that reason. No common room to pass through; fewer people to spot the king. "A good choice," I said, and managed to keep a strangled tone out of my voice.

Once night had fully fallen, we put up our hoods and departed.

We'd gotten no more than five paces up the street when they came at us. Cloaked and hooded men, they emerged from the shadows beside the tavern door, they ran from the alley mouth across the street, they leaped from a wagon loaded with bags of seed, a dozen and more. As they neared us they threw back their hoods and cloaks to reveal the uniforms of municipal guards. They carried swords, some of them crossbows.

I got my sword out a bare second after Viriat readied his. Jerno drew and stepped over so the three of us stood in a curved line, Viriat left, me center, Jerno right, with Halleyne and Jenina and the tavern wall behind us.

I heard a scrambling and glanced back. Jenina was climbing the ceramic drainpipe that ran up the tavern wall. Though hampered by shoes, she climbed like a jungle monkey and quickly scampered onto the flat rooftop.

"Stop in the name of the Crown," called the most heavily decorated of the guards, a bearded man, a captain by his markings. His tone was odd, more courteous and conciliatory than I would have expected.

"Halleyne!" That was Jenina. I glanced again and saw her extending her hand down for my wife. But in front of us the crossbowmen were bringing up their weapons. If Halleyne tried to climb, she'd be slaughtered by their quarrels.

"Go," I told Jenina. And as two of the crossbowmen brought their weapons to bear, she did just that, dropping flat to the rooftop and rolling away out of their sight.

The captain, seeing her departure, sighed. He continued his approach until he was within range of Jerno's broadsword, but did not bring his own sword on guard. "Jerno Byriver, King of Lieda, I am required by the queen your wife to bring you before her. I want no struggle. A fight will cost me men, cost you companions, and cost us all time, and when all was done you would still be standing before the queen."

The king glared at him. "Another reasonable man. I am sick of reasonable men." But he handed over his sword, and Viriat and I sullenly followed suit.

Chapter Six

The night was not too much older when it found us in the royal citadel's private reception hall, the waiting room outside the royal quarters. It was a long hall with white marble columns and a speckled-green marble floor, paintings of deceased royal ancestors and their favorite horses on the walls, a bare minimum of furniture—mostly delicate chairs and spindly-legged couches upholstered in green velvet.

I'd spent many hours in this very room, coordinating with the other royal servants so that the king's wardrobe and accoutrements matched both his mood and his day's duties. Today the king's wardrobe was a set of commoner's garments that had once belonged to an uncle of mine; he looked very out of place perched on one of the delicate chairs. In addition to the two door guards protecting the inner quarters, there was one citadel guard for each of us.

"Do you suppose she's redecorated?" I asked King Jerno.

"Kin, you're resuming your annoying ways."

"No, truly. She always hated the drapes you'd chosen for the royal bed and that tapestry of the Battle of Fairy Bridge. I bet they're all gone."

He glowered but did not rise to the baiting I'd hoped would distract him. Halleyne, seated on the couch beside me, gave me a sympathetic smile.

The inner doors opened. First to emerge were two more citadel guards, carrying with them the queen's portable throne, a beautifully carved and padded wooden chair that was barely light enough for two muscular men to haul between them. They set it down in the center of the room.

"Ah," said Jerno. "We're to get the Official Private Audience For Those Who Have Made Her Unhappy."

Viriat and I rose. Halleyne followed suit. Jerno stayed seated. Royal servants brought out a small oval carpet to place before the throne and a small side table upon which they placed beside the right arm; this they littered with accoutrements such as a fan, perfumes, and kerchiefs.

I told the king, "She's prepared for us to stink." Jerno nodded. "I taught her that one."

The servants withdrew and the queen emerged between two more guards.

She was a tall woman, dark of complexion and eye, with hair like spun silk dyed the hue of the blackest night. When last I'd seen her, moons ago, she was a tired woman, beaten down by the loss of three sons and of her youth, wasted away watching a war eat the spirit and resources of her kingdom. But now she looked as she had when I'd first seen her up close: erect and proud, like a hawk transformed by the gods into a woman, a slim beauty with the carriage of majesty.

She ignored us while she seated herself and arranged her robes to her liking. I found it interesting that the guards did not force Jerno to stand for her arrival. That, and the fact that there was no herald's announcement of the queen's arrival, meant he was being treated as a royal prisoner of rank, and one who was in the queen's confidence, not as the imposter the notices had claimed he was.

Queen Elowar finally deigned to notice her visitors; she looked between us. "Sit, please. Jerno. Viriat. Kin. And you must be *Thalahai* Halleyne."

"I am. Health and contentment to Your Majesty."

"Do you represent your queen before me?"

"I do. My papers of introduction were among the things your guards removed from us."

Along with our weapons. Including both my knives.

"They will be returned. I regret to inform you that they are meaningless unless your queen resumes her throne."

"Thank you, Majesty." Halleyne sounded polite but unconcerned.

Elowar returned her attention to the king. "I understand from another visitor that you have, during our long separation, put me from you. Divorced me."

Interesting. There was to be no preamble. No exchange of pleasantries or sweet-coated insults.

Jerno nodded glumly. "Something I did in a moment of madness."

"Would you undo it, then?"

"If it would please you."

"But not to please yourself."

"To please myself, yes, if you can answer me something in the affirmative."

"Ask."

He took a moment to compose his words. "It has taken me moons of restored sensibility to understand what I owe you. Faithfulness. Strong sons. Good counsel. Knowing you would always array your allies and political favors behind my decisions even when you questioned them. But I think there is no doubt between us that affection faded to nothingness over the years. I thought I felt you grow to hate me when our third son died."

"Died. You mean, killed himself over love of a foreign prisoner *you* ordered impaled."

"Even some of my advisors recommended her swift execution, Elowar. And Tarno died, too, from his own sense of honor. Yes. That's exactly what I mean. And now I have hurt you again. What I ask is this. If that was hatred, has it left you? If you believe that divorce came from my madness, do you believe that madness has fled? If I put aside this divorce, can you be my partner as before in the times to come?"

She hesitated not a moment. "No." There was steel behind her gaze.

"Then I would not undo it."

They looked at one another a long moment and I thought I could see the last delicate ribbons of their union part and snap between them.

"I am a woman of honor, Jerno."

"I know."

"I will not lie to Lieda and say you are an imposter. But that does not mean you can come here and leap into your throne. I will give you a choice. You will go before the Council of Judges to be recognized, and resume your throne, and I will abdicate so that you can choose another queen. Or I can have you put to death for the many hurts you have given me, in which case the Council of Judges and your old supporters will condemn, exile, perhaps execute me for regicide."

Jerno's tone became guarded. "One would think that my best choice would be to resume my throne."

"Yes. But I place conditions upon it."

"Ah."

"You will grant me rule of Marketry Province and grant it the status of full principality."

The city of Marketry, an important waystation for sea traffic to the west, was almost as far from Bekalli as one could get and yet remain within Lieda.

"And?"

"And you will set your royal signature and seal to all treaties, declarations, and proclamations I have made in your absence."

"And?"

"And I will choose your heir. Heir to the throne of Lieda."

He looked surprised. "Whom would you choose?"

She shrugged. "I do not know yet. You will grant me in document the right to choose your royal heir. If I die, my own heir will have that choice to make. If the heir I choose for you dies, and I die, and my heirs all die, so no one is left to inherit this right, then the Council of Judges will choose your heir. But—" Her voice became harsh, cutting. "—your heir may not be of your descent.

Lieda will never again be ruled by one who might inherit your taint of madness."

I felt a sense of unreality come over me. It was interesting to watch the queen try to drive a stake into history, changing forever the way things would be done.

The king let no emotion touch his face. "And?"

"That is all."

"I will consider this."

"You have until this audience is ended. At that time, if no answer is forthcoming, I will have you executed." The queen turned to the rest of us. "Kin, I hope you understand, if I have the king killed, your judgeship will not be confirmed."

I chuckled without meaning to. "Is that the worst I have to worry about?"

"Yes. I will bring you no harm. I think you have done well. I heard of the way you worked to restore reason to my husband's mind. I see you have married well."

That brought a smile to my lips. "I am pleased you are pleased. But Majesty, I have concerns for some of the political alliances you have made. I do not question your ability, but to my certain knowledge lies have been placed before you like walls—"

"You're speaking of Sheroit dar Bontine and Teuper Hiaran."

"I am. They were shipwrecked among us . . . and have obviously denied being there. They were part of the conspiracy that stranded us . . . and again must have denied their complicity. Now they represent two of the nations founded partly out of territories you have surrendered."

"You are wrong, Kin, and are entitled to the

truth, which I had from King Sheroit's own lips not long ago."

"I would be happy to be enlightened."

"Teuper is, of course, son and heir of King Jehan Hiaran. But he was raised mostly in Terosalle, sent down from the mountains by his father so he would learn the gentility of the courts. And Jehan has long planned to unite the mountain tribes into a true nation.

"On the last day of your treaty expedition, while your ships were still at anchor, Teuper asked Sheroit to row with him out a distance from the ships that they might not be overheard while he discussed the mountain situation with him. Teuper and his father wanted Sheroit's help in wringing concessions of mountain land from the courts of Lieda and Terosalle."

"I see."

"So it was when the storms overtook you. Sheroit and Teuper were blown to another isle, much closer to Feyndala, and their little boat was wrecked. And among the storm-spirits that shipwrecked you all were other things—double-spirits—who swarmed down upon them and assumed their forms."

Double-spirits. Liedan folklore was full of stories of these spirits, who took the forms of blameless people and ruined their lives while they were away on honest business. I'd always thought that these stories were in actuality warnings for traveling men and women to leave someone behind to spy on their families and friends.

"These spirits," she continued, "mocked them and hurt them and told them they would make tatters of their sterling reputations, then flew off into the departing storm. They must have been sent by whatever malignant force also sent the storms that shipwrecked you."

"I see. So Sheroit contends it was his double and Teuper's that lived among us, not the men themselves."

"Certainly. Do the actions Zilona described of Sheroit match his deeds of the past?"

Yes, they do. His whole life has been one of a manipulator who cannot stop himself from manipulation. I sighed. I could not tell her that. Could not tell her that the story was obviously the fabrication of a man who feared, perhaps sensed, that others might make it alive off Landfall. But a little nagging voice inside me wondered if the story were true.

Of course, I had a way to find out. I'd stabbed the Teuper who was shipwrecked with us. If Prince Teuper of Hiaraniard bore my stab wound, the story was a lie. I felt a little more at peace knowing that I could put a hole in his story as easily as I'd put a hole in him.

"At any rate," the queen continued, "because of your devotion to duty on the island, neither you nor your family has aught to worry about."

"My family?"

"I know General Underbridge sheltered you last night when he should have reported the king's return. That is clear sign his loyalty is to Jerno rather than to me. But I will seek no revenge against him."

I thought back over Zilona's letter. "How long did it take to break the girl?"

That caught the attention of my other companions.

"Not long," the queen said. "She was a lady-in-waiting, not a soldier. She told all."

"So she is not now on a carriage bound for the Terosai capital."

"No. She has betrayed her queen and our king; she lied to me when I asked her direct questions about Jerno's whereabouts last night; she declined to help us locate your Landfall islands on the charts because she correctly feared that I would arrange to have her fellow Terosai brought here as prisoners. All at first. After she broke, we were able to locate your islands—they are properly the Melthue Chain, and known from old maps of those parts. By the way, Jerno, all military ships in Bekalli Harbor of any size have been denied permission to sail. No matter which of your old captains you might have gotten to, there will be no other rescue than the one I am sending."

So she didn't know of our alternate plan, the hiring of a merchant. I thought back on our discussions. Zilona hadn't been privy to all our planning sessions.

Elowar spread her hands, a gesture of reasonability. "And Zilona is to be executed."

"No!" Viriat rose, but a guard placed the point of a sword to his throat and forced him down. "Majesty, if you feel any appreciation at all for the duties I have performed for you—"

"Of course I do. But the girl must die. Of all her crimes, the one that cannot be condoned is the betrayal of my husband to forces she thought would harm him."

Jerno scowled at her. "I will abandon thoughts of vengeance against her."

"I will not."

"Then let us place her on the table. What do you want for her?"

"I will not trade for her. She dies."

"I will decree her a pardon."

"By all means, do so. And when you are king again, it will take effect. Of course, she will have been dead for days or weeks by then, but she will at least not be a criminal."

"Elowar, why?"

"For our son. For Tarno."

The king shook his head, not understanding.

"You killed him, Jerno. You sped the execution of the girl he loved. You convinced him that you could only be made aware of your own failings as a king if he took drastic steps. So he did. He took his own life. And you still did not understand."

"That has nothing to do with Zilona."

"It has everything to do with her. You say you are no longer mad. That is good. So you will feel this. You will know the girl has died and it is your fault. You will know that Viriat was fond of her and will never be able to abandon the hate he feels for you because your deeds led to her death. Because you have finally cost yourself so much that your mind is again keen, she will hover around you like a ghost for the rest of your life. This is a revenge I can have on you, for no greater price than executing one who would have harmed you." She settled back, no doubt in her expression. "This was a suggestion of Minister Gastin's. A good one. A high yield for a small cost."

"Gastin! It was he who said I should impale that Terosai princess Tarno loved. You question his recommendation to me but accept his recommendation to you?"

"In this case, yes."

I cleared my throat. "Majesty—"

"No, Kin," she said. "Be still."

And still we all were: me held in place by the queen's words; the king, his face paling, held by the helplessness of his situation; Viriat kept in check by the sword point an inch from his throat; Halleyne kept still by the very good sense she exhibited every day of her life.

The king said, "I accept."

"Eh?"

"Your offer. I accept."

"Good. You will all be installed in royal apartments. So will that sailor woman when she is found. Jerno, Viriat, you may not leave yours until Jerno is recognized by the Council of Judges and resumes his throne. In the meantime Jerno may occupy himself signing the proclamations and treaties brought down to his room. On the day the judges recognize him, he will be king and I will be but a former queen. Kin, Halleyne, you may do whatever you wish, but the girl dies tomorrow before my departure and if you do anything to prevent it you will find your disloyal father in great difficulty."

She rose, and we all did too, save Jerno.

"Your departure?" I asked. "I am surprised you leave the capital at such a time. Mind you, that's not criticism."

The queen smiled as though her good humor were magically restored. "I leave for events taking place at Mount Rozinki."

"Rozinki? Rather an awkward name. Foreign."

"It used to be Mount Preskon. Now King Jehan builds his citadel and capital there. I go to witness the wedding of Queen Thaliara and Captain Buyan. General Buyan now; he's a commander of Terosai forces. Oh, Jerno, have you anything you wish me to say to this other son of yours?"

The king thought about it. "No."

Mount Preskon. That brought back memories for me. The Western Trade Route, a series of game trails and mountain passes strung together by road-builders in ancient times, crossed north-south through the mountains between Lieda and Terosalle. Another trail paralleled the Route for many day-marches in distance, and it is at the center point of this second trail that Mount Preskon lies. Years ago, I accompanied Prince Balaquin, who was an engineer, to that selfsame point to commence the construction of a fortress to mark the border between the nations. It was there that we met a Terosai attack force, an elite unit. While I fled back to the nearest outpost, Balaquin and his engineers retreated before the enemy army, slowing it the crucial few days I needed . . . but he died of exposure in so doing. I knew the mountain well, and odds were good that King Jehan's citadel was being built on the foundations Balaquin's engineers laid down.

The queen swept out of the room during my voyage into memory. The doors closed behind her.

We had a few private moments to talk, huddled in a corner of the hall, while the palace major-domo arranged for us to be quartered.

Viriat said, "You and the Lady Halleyne have

freedom of movement. Kin, you must save Zilona." There was strain in his voice.

"I don't know if I can. We've little time." My mind galloped like a racehorse but arrived at no answer. "Viriat, she betrayed you. She betrayed all of us."

"I know. Must she die for it?"

"So, you love her, then?"

"I . . . do." He hung his head, not, I think, embarrassed by his words, but ashamed of the weakness he had demonstrated by begging.

My lady spoke up. "King Jerno, how old is the queen?"

The king calculated. "Our son Jernin was born when she was eighteen, he'd now be three-and-thirty if he had lived . . . so, one-and-fifty. Why do you ask?"

"Her hands and neck were firm. Smooth. There were almost no wrinkles at the corners of her eyes. Did you not notice?"

"I noticed she looked very appealing. I reluctantly attributed it to our moons of separation."

She shook her head. "It was more than that."

I said, "This is something my lady-wife knows a great deal about. If she's certain that the queen benefits from more than makeup, you can stake your life on her opinion."

Then the guards returned.

Halleyne and I waited only seconds in the sumptuous quarters the guards took us to. Then we emerged into the hall again and caught those guards before they departed. "Please take us to the royal prison," I told them.

The chief guard, who had been with us in the

reception hall, looked uncomfortable. "The queen's directive was that you were to take no step to free the prisoner—"

"Ah!" I gave him my coldest smile. "Did I say, come help us free the prisoner?"

"No."

"Did the queen say, don't let them *speak* with the prisoner?"

"No."

"Well?"

"This way."

As we were conducted down to the ground floor, Halleyne leaned close and whispered, "You were stabbing before he knew it was a fight."

"I've barely begun. I think it's more important that I be a harsh, nasty Judge Underbridge now. As long as they continue to think of me as the king's valet, they will offer me little but condescension."

"I understand."

As we reached the ground floor, among the crowd of people generally to be found milling in the foyer just within the palace doors I saw courtiers and functionaries I recognized. I waved jauntily to one of them—Tarraskin Cutter, a messenger. He saw me, nodded, glanced away, then looked again and came tearing after us. "Kin! Is it you?"

"It is."

He caught up with us but did not approach too closely; we were being conducted by guards, after all. "I thought you were dead."

"I'm not."

"With the king."

"He lives, too."

That stopped him in his tracks; he stared at us as we passed outside into the great courtyard.

"So you seek to complicate things with rumors," Halleyne whispered.

"I do. The more little fires the queen has to put out, the more sneakiness we may be able to get away with."

"Have I said recently that I admire the devious pathways of your mind?"

"Not for a day or two, no."

The guards marched us past the low square wall that defends the palace to the dark gray-stone building that served it as prison for the most important—and the most hated—prisoners. Once inside, at my request, Halleyne told the captain on duty, "We are here to see the prisoner Zilona dar Machias."

The captain gave her a stern look, which she returned. He said, "There is no such prisoner on my records."

"Whatever name she's been given, or none, she's the special prisoner of the queen, given over to you earlier today. A Terosai woman."

"Your name?"

"*Thalahai* Halleyne Underbridge, special emissary—since a moon ago—of Lia dar Kothia Surdosti, Queen of Terosalle. And lady of Judge Kin Underbridge."

Well done, I thought. *More rumors for dispersal.*

The captain looked at our guards, who nodded, and personally conducted us down to the basement levels of the prison.

A bad sign. This was not the place for well-received prisoners. The halls and cells were hacked out of living stone, with slats of heavy iron and steel making up the cell bars; this region of the prison was a fortress. The place stank so of human filth that one could not smell odors of blood, sweat, and sickness beneath them. Halleyne held my kerchief over her nose.

The end of one stone corridor widened; in the broad open area was a table where sat another guard, and all around were heavy oaken doors with small barred windows, a half-dozen of them. The captain pointed at one. "That's her," he said.

Through the little window I could see, barely visible on a shadowy corner cot, the slight figure of a woman.

"Dismissed," Halleyne said. The captain glowered at her, then marched away, his shoulders stiff.

I turned to the guard on duty. "Open it."

"You have her papers of release?"

"No, you idiot, we're not here to free her. My lady wants to speak to her." I saw Zilona jerk at the sound of my voice. She raised her head from the cot and turn tear-streaked eyes toward us.

The guard rose to unlock the door, obviously very put-upon by these unnecessary visitors. When Halleyne entered he locked the door behind her.

"Still scheduled for execution tomorrow?" I asked him.

"Yes, yes."

"Did you question her yourself?"

"Yes, yes. Some of the time. I was there for all the questioning."

"Good! Tell me everything she said of Queen Lia."

Did I need to hear anything she'd said of Queen

Lia? No. But it would distract the guards so they
might pay little or no attention to Halleyne; and
when our activities were reported, the first and
perhaps only thing they would recall from this
was my abiding interest in Zilona's words about
the deposed Terosai queen.

So he told me things I had heard dozens of times
about that queen's petty jealousies, cruel punish-
ments, and vanities. I'd married one woman who
had served her, and was the friend of another; there
was nothing new here, but I dutifully nodded and
asked probing questions about the man's perceptions
of the truthfulness of her answers. Gradually he got
into the spirit of it, explaining how he knew by the
timber of her voice and, damn him, how fast she
answered after the lash fell whether her words were
true or not.

Eventually my wife rapped to be released and
the guard let her rejoin me. His face was pale
and as perfectly still as a windless bay.

"They've lashed her back open," she whispered
into my ear, almost spitting in anger.

As the jailer locked the door again, I said, "See
to it she has a doctor visit tonight."

"No need," he said. "She dies in the morning."

I took the back of his head and pushed, slamming his forehead into the bars of the door. With
my other hand I yanked the knife free from his
belt and held its point to his neck. Then I swung
him around until he was between me and the
palace guards, who were just reaching for their
own weapons.

"Do you know my name?" I asked my prisoner.
He was bleeding copiously from the forehead,
blinking to get the red stuff out of his eyes.

"Yes, sir. Underbridge, sir."

"And my title?"

"No, sir."

"Judge. I can convict you this moment of crimes you just confessed to me."

The other guards looked at one another. I could tell what was in their minds: If I were attempting a prison break, I was going about it in a very odd way.

"And do you know my age?"

"No, sir."

"Five-and-twenty. I'm the youngest high judge in Lieda. In the last year, I've stabbed a man to death in a fair fight, put down a rebellion against your king, fomented another one, and killed more deadly serpents than you can count. I'm not like any judge you've ever seen. And do you know what?"

"What, sir?"

"If that prisoner does not see a physician this night, I will be very, very unhappy with you." I pushed him into the door again, hard, then extended a hand for Halleyne.

She declined for a moment. When the jailer had removed himself from the door and staggered to his table, shooting me lethal glares, she took his place at the little barred window and called, "Zilona."

The prisoner came to the window a moment later and they exchanged very quiet words. Then my lady took her place at my side. Arm in arm, we peaceably walked past the palace guards; I showed them both hands to prove I was no longer armed.

"I saw that," Halleyne whispered, struggling unsuccessfully with a smile.

"You saw what?"

"I saw you put that knife up your sleeve."

"An old habit. I'm so ashamed. What else did you see?"

"Stone walls, tight grates, stout bars, and a very frightened girl. Foolish, foolish child. I saw no way out for her. Until, that is, you ruined the face of that revolting jailer."

"That inspired you? Gave you an idea for rescue?"

"Oh, yes."

"I'm to hammer her door down with a succession of jailers' heads?"

She just smiled.

Chapter Seven

The first knock came mere minutes after our return to our assigned chambers. "Who comes?" I called.

The man outside answered, "General Haythan Oakwall."

I smiled at my wife. "Chief commander of His Majesty's armies. A good start." I answered, "Enter!"

The door opened for the lean, gray figure of General Oakwall. Well I knew him; he was a frequent visitor to my father's house, and he and my father had traded the duties of chief commander a couple of times during their careers. He was better at political management than my sire, hence his survival as commander when my father was relegated to pensioner, but he was a good man nonetheless. I liked the way he rewarded his common soldiers for jobs well done and the way he wore plain, unadorned uniforms when among them. As he was dressed today; he still had dust on his boots.

I took his proffered hand. "General Oakwall. You never tire."

He smiled. "I hear it's *Judge* Underbridge now. On that, and your survival of course, I congratulate you."

I gestured to Halleyne. "Allow me to introduce my lady-wife, *Thalahai* Halleyne Underbridge. You may speak freely before her, for I tell her everything I hear anyway, and she is as loyal as I." Loyal to what, I did not say.

He did not visibly react to her Terosai ancestry; either he'd already heard and schooled himself, or did not care. He gave her a little bow before returning his attention to me. "Is it true?" he asked.

"Yes."

"You didn't ask me what I meant. That's not like you, Kin."

"But I know what you meant! Is it true the king lives? Yes. Is it true that he and the queen have arranged a divorce, a parting of rights and titles and wealth? Yes. Though you really should ask the king and queen about those details."

"They aren't taking visitors!"

"Ah. Here. Sit. Would you care for wine?" Over the general's head, I gave Halleyne a scowl. She'd been right about the royals not seeing even their confidants, so she had scored a point on me. She gave me a little smile of victory.

"Yes, please. Dust from here to Soort's Hill clogs my throat." He gratefully accepted the goblet Halleyne handed him and drained half its contents. "Here's to survival, then. A time for celebration."

Halleyne and I shook our heads in unison. "Rather," she said, "a time for mourning."

"Whomever for?"

"The girl," I said.

"Which girl?"

"The Terosai girl the queen has sentenced to die tomorrow morning," Halleyne said.

"The girl King Jerno would really rather survive," I said.

The general's head whipped back and forth as he tracked from my lady to me. "Who is she? What is she to him?"

"I can't say," Halleyne said.

"Nor I," I said. "Forbidden." *Don't ask by whom, general.*

"On the other hand," Halleyne said, "General Oakwall is renowned for his cleverness. His tactical wisdom."

"True," I said. It wasn't true. He was renowned for being able to inspire his troops to rage and courage and sacrifice . . . and for understanding that his field officers had tactical abilities superior to his. "I'm sure he can assemble the pieces and arrive at his own answer."

"Certainly," she said. "You already know the facts, General. Liedans and Terosai stranded together on that tiny little island. Some fighting. Some falling in love." She smiled again at me.

"The king returns to Feyndala in the company of a lovely, unwed Terosai girl from a good family," I said. "A day later, the queen captures them, divorces the king in a rage, has the girl beaten and then sentences her to death."

"I know what *I'd* conclude," my wife said. "More wine?"

"Yes, please."

"I just wish I had some good men and some coin for bribes," I said. "I could turn them into great favors and fortune."

"How?" the general asked.

"I'd—" I looked around suspiciously. We'd already been talking in low tones, the habit of people familiar with visitors' quarters in royal palaces and their often perforated walls. I dropped my voice still lower. "I'd rescue the girl, of course."

"King Jerno will resume his throne in a week or two," Halleyne said. "I think, then, that someone near to his throne would be *very* grateful if that girl Zilona turned up alive."

"I wish I could collect that reward," I said. "More wine?"

When, finally, the door closed behind General Oakwall, I took Halleyne in my arms. "You were right," I said.

"Say that again."

"You were right, you were right. The desire of people to please those who are about to come to power is very strong. Sometimes tricky to harness, but strong." I kissed her, but someone rapped on the door. "Damn it. Who comes?"

A new voice, raspy and aged, answered, "Chief Judge Olam Byriver."

"The king's cousin," I whispered. "Another good one." I raised my voice: "Enter and be welcome!"

Halleyne whispered, "We're going to need more wine."

In the earliest part of the morning, when the sun had itself not yet clambered out of its bed, I heard many rushing footsteps in the corridor outside our room. I got up and padded as silently as I could to stand beside my door—beside the rug I'd laid there before undressing for the night. When someone outside said, "Open it," I took the edge of the rug in both hands.

The door swung in, admitting light and a handful of palace guardsmen. I gave the rug a ferocious yank and was rewarded by seeing all six guards tumble to the marble floor.

Then I was on them, seizing a polearm that had fallen from the hand of one, laying about me, beating the heads of the fallen with the polearm shaft and shouting "Help! Guards! We are attacked! Assassins!"

"Kin!" That was the queen, entering the room behind her honor guard. "Stop that at once! These *are* the guards."

I looked at her stupidly. "Oh." Then I handed the polearm back to its owner, helped him up, helped another guard up, deftly removed the hip-cloak from the back of the captain and wrapped it around my nakedness, all the while saying, "I'm sorry, I'm sorry. I hope you understand. Roused suddenly from sleep, clashing arms, doors bursting in—you really should knock. Had I my sword back, this would have been a frightful waste of palace guards."

A lie, most of it. Halleyne and I had hardly slept through the night, but our weary, hollow-eyed appearances would at least lend credence to the story that we were just awakened. While I spoke, Halleyne got the bedside lamp lit and looked at us with feigned drowsiness from the bed.

The queen asked, "Kin, did you do it?"

"Did I do what?"

"Break the girl out of the royal prison."

I let my eyes widen. "Gods, no. I've been in this very room since we saw her last night. Except for a side-trip to get food and wine for an endless parade of royal visitors."

I could tell she was not satisfied with my answer.

"I want you to swear it, Kin. I think you still have some respect for matters of honor and for your family name."

I didn't have to pretend to be angry then. I drew myself up to my full height and glowered. "As you wish. I, Kin Underbridge, judge of Lieda, on my oath and on my name, swear before the gods that I did not rescue the prisoner Zilona, did not attempt to rescue the prisoner Zilona, did not conspire to rescue the prisoner Zilona." *Don't ask about inciting a rescue, Majesty.*

"You said nothing of inciting her rescue."

Damn. She always was quick. I looked up to the skies, as if thinking that only the gods could hammer some sense into this queen, then returned my attention to her, leaning so close that our noses almost touched—I could feel rather than see her guards becoming restless with my motion. "Your Majesty, were I to have incited someone to a crime, I think I would then know who did it. So to answer your next question: I add to my oath, under the same terms and circumstances, that I have no knowledge of the identity of the rescuer or rescuers."

She looked into my eyes—deep as I'd seen her sometimes do with a fibbing son—and her expression softened. "I am glad. I had no wish to visit justice on you." She gestured to her somewhat battered guards. "Come." And she swept out again with them in tow. I closed the door behind them.

Immediately there was a little knock. I took the hip-cloak from around my middle, opened the door a handspan, and handed the garment out. It was snatched away and I closed the door again.

Halleyne was laughing when I rejoined her in

bed. "The sight of my naked husband bouncing about, battering the helmets of royal guards and crying for help—"

"All for your amusement."

She sobered. "You are growing quite militant about making them treat you with the respect due a judge."

"Not in this case. I arranged to beat their helmets in for disrespect to *you*, dear heart. No one comes crashing in on my sleeping wife while I'm here to prevent it. Or at least make them suffer for it."

She gave me another smile, quite pleased.

"By the way, you were right."

"About what?" she asked.

"The queen. She's the age of my mother. And yet when I got a close look at her just now, that seemed impossible. She appears to be our age."

"She's done something." Halleyne looked fretful. "I wish I knew what." She brightened. "Zilona got away."

"Yes, she did. Your plan was a brilliant success; I have married a very sneaky wife. And if Zilona remembers to do as you told her—lets her rescuer continue to think she is the king's new favorite—she will survive to be reunited with Viriat. We have done a lifetime's worth of good deed for that wretched, ungrateful girl, and it's finally time to see to ourselves."

"We have plans for today?"

"I'm afraid so, and they start early."

As we passed out of the citadel's western gates Halleyne said, "I sang last night."

"I heard you as I drifted in and out of sleep. A bright, merry tune. What was it?"

" 'The Spring Hunting Song.' 'Along the banks the maids go streaming/seeking lads who lie a-dreaming/ dancing river waters swirling/by the banks the maids go twirling . . . '—it's a dancing song."

"It's a springtime find-a-willing-partner-and-sneak-off-into-the-bushes song."

"That, too. But it doesn't matter. I wasn't actually singing."

"I feel myself becoming lost in the whirlpool of your logic. What were you doing, then?"

"Practicing magic. The song is about hunting among many, seeking the right one. I was using it as a basis for spirit-magic. I was looking for spirits, as an exercise. I was hoping to find Shallia's spirit floating in search of me, but I also thought that, surely, in a palace as big and old as this one, with court magicians and a history of treachery and deceit—"

"Just treachery. They are mere apprentices at deceit."

"—that there would be other spirits about I could feel."

"Were there? You sound troubled."

"Yes, there were. And as before, I could feel them hear my song, feel them respond to my song, even direct them a little—come hither, go back—with emotion and intent."

"But."

"Yes, but. But there was a cluster of them, three I think, and fairly close, that felt different. I could not move them. I do not even think they heard me. They were trapped, immobile . . . screaming in silence."

"Someone punished by a court magician for some ancient crime, perhaps?"

"Not ancient. There was the air of freshness to them. They were recently come to their fate, I think." Her voice was troubled and I took her hand.

"Once our other problems are settled, we will look into it," I promised her.

"So, what is our first errand?"

"We're going to buy you a mirror."

I sold a gold ring I'd slipped from the hand of the dazed guard-captain as I was helping him up. Then, at an armorer's, I bought a club—a good, stout piece of oak, not costly, the sort of thing a boy from a poor family buys when tapped to join the army of a war in progress.

Then, in the street market close to the harbor, I found the stand I wanted; on its many display planks were arrayed combs, mirrors, little pots of creams, and other articles of a lady's toilet.

I bought a good-sized mirror; its face was of silver, not the more recent glass-and-silver meldings. "That's the one. I want you to admire yourself in that for some time. And move about a bit."

"And what will you be doing?"

"Walking about in a circle and watching you . . . and trying to spot any palace flunky assigned to follow you."

"Ah. And what will I be doing?"

"Spotting whatever palace flunky has been assigned to follow me. And then signaling me."

"Ah. How will I signal you?"

I gave her a stern look.

"Oh, of course. I must be addled by the morning hour."

I gave her a kiss and then dashed along the

line of stands. Of course, "dashed" is a relative term; the street, already thick with sellers and buyers, was not the ideal place for a sprint. But I moved as fast as the crowd allowed, got to the end of one line of stands, turned that corner, and trotted back the way I'd come on the other side.

I got to a spot where a furrier's stand spanned the double row of stands. I could see through it to the other side and spotted my wife, who was now the very model of a vapid court lady endlessly admiring herself. But she'd turned around so her mirror could catch the sun, and was playing light on a small group of men who had already passed her.

No, just one man. When the fellow, a young man in an innocuous cloak, broke free of the pack, the reflection she was aiming bounced to him.

I looked at the crowd around my wife and back a good distance from her. Many were looking at her, either because of her beauty or her self-indulgent antics . . . but none I saw was stationary. So the palace had only assigned one guard to the two of us. I felt miffed.

I grabbed the sleeve of the next passerby who was about my size. "Would you like to earn a good woolen cloak and a silver penny for doing almost nothing?" I asked.

"Is this a trick?"

"Not this time." I swept the cloak from about my shoulders and onto his, then fished a silver coin from my pouch. "Put the hood up and walk in that direction at a steady pace for a hundred steps and you'll have earned them both." I gave him a pat on the back and set him into motion. Then I crowded close to a booth and pretended to be absorbed in the study of ground spices.

My young pursuer rounded the turn I'd made a while back. He cast about for a few moments, then spotted the fellow I'd given the cloak to and hurried after him.

I felt a moment of regret as he came close. Such a young, handsome guardsman, just doing the dictates of his queen and captain . . . then I stepped out of my position of concealment and rammed the butt of the club into his chest, driving the wind out of him.

He looked surprised.

I took the club by the handle and swung it into his crotch. I saw him take on an expression of something like grief in the brief moment before the blow landed. Then it hit. His face changed color and he fell over.

I noticed that many of the people about were staring at me. So I shouted down at the luckless fellow, "And don't you ever look at my wife again!" And I left to the sound of their applause.

"Such a dear husband," Halleyne said when I rejoined her. "Always protecting my honor."

"You heard that?"

"They probably heard it back at the palace. You bellow, dear. Do I get to keep the mirror?"

"Of course."

The berth of the *Driftwood* was empty. So we went on to the harbormaster's office and talked to the clerk. "That berth, opposite the blue-shuttered inn at Blackstone Way—is it available?"

The clerk rummaged through his papers. "That

would be Blackstone Four. Yes. *Driftwood* settled and sailed . . . just before dawn, in fact."

"Delightful. I'll tell my captain." We left in high spirits; the rescue expedition was on its way.

Then, a physician. We found one whose clients were mostly the women of well-heeled trader and merchant families. She examined Halleyne and pronounced her healthy, though a little ill-nourished, and said our baby would be born in late fall. As we departed, the physician chided me to keep my wife fed.

Then, the most important errand of all, a proper magician. We went to their guild hall to consult the licenses of registered practitioners and I found the names of those who had greater knowledge of the sort of evil influences that can affect children born and unborn.

Master Tangorn Hillfoot was old but not elderly, lean but not frail. His beard was so pure a white that I was sure he had to bleach it with his arts, and his eyes, a clear blue, bespoke intelligence. Too, he was friendly. Perhaps I was irrational in my protectiveness of Halleyne, but I did not want her to be poked or prodded by anyone unsympathetic. We told him the whole story of our exile, omitting very little.

"I'd not believe a word," he said, "if rumor had not already floated down from the palace that the king still lives."

"That's harder to believe than a snake-goddess beneath a sunken volcano and serpents with spirits in their venom?" Halleyne asked.

"Of course. Gods and spirits do as they please. Men and women seldom come back from being declared dead."

He subjected Halleyne to a variety of tests. She drank a brew of ale and spices and then spat three times—with all delicacy—on a silver platter dusted with powder; each little bit of spittle changed to a different color. She sang to a feather sealed inside a glass jar and was delighted when it rose and danced to her song. He had her bare her bosom and abdomen, earning scowls from me, and then held a rose-colored glass funnel to her flesh, tapping the funnel in many places with a painted wooden stick. Then, later, he held the funnel there again and had her sing to it, cycles of notes that did not make up a song, until she found a sequence that would make the funnel ring with a single pure note.

When all that was done he had Halleyne lace herself, then he sat us down; I saw with hopefulness that his expression was not grave. "Well, you are with child," he said.

Halleyne smiled. "I know that."

"And the child is, as you suspected, different."

Her smile faded. "In what way?"

"In ways both good and bad, my lady. The child is open, receptive to the flow of magic. I think he will be a most intuitive magician or perhaps Bard. Perhaps very powerful as well."

I said, "That's obviously the good side of the coin."

He nodded. "And the bad. His very receptiveness is a danger. He is far more vulnerable to, well, intrusion. By spirits, by malevolent forces. To possession."

Halleyne reached out her hand for me and I took it. "Will he always be this way?"

"Well . . . no. As a youth he can be trained

to shield himself. As an adult he may be a master
at it. But as a child he will need all the help you
can give him." From a shelf, the magician fetched
a piece of carved blue stone on a string. When
it stopped swinging I could make it out: it was
a comical, naked, roly-poly man sticking his tongue
out. "This is your first defense."

"You're joking," I said. Halleyne took the little
icon from him.

"No. Silly as it seems, that is a ward. Its very
pose and manner say 'go away.' The choice of
stone and enchantments spoken over it during its
carving reinforce that meaning . . . a meaning
spirits can sense. My lady, wear it on a chain or
cord about your neck until the child is born. And
once or twice a day, sing to your child the notes
we have learned together; they are a slap in the
face of any malignancy that has sensed your child
and hovers about it. And come back to me
often—once a moon would be good. Do all these
things, and more as we learn them, and your child
will be fine." He shrugged. "There's nothing more
to be done today. Go forth, remain healthy, do
as I've said. All will be well."

"Thank you, sir," I said. "What is our debt to
you?"

"Nothing. With her music and her natural
aptitude, your wife has taught *me* something today.
I intend to learn more. Fair warning: as she
returns to me for visits, I'm going to persuade
her to apprentice herself to me."

"Fair warning: if you do, she'll become master
of this establishment."

As we left, I turned back to him. "You said,
he will be a most intuitive magician."

He smacked himself in the forehead. "I did. That's not the sort of secret I remind myself to keep."

I smiled and we departed.

When we were outside, Halleyne swayed and leaned against me. I held her upright. "Halleyne? Are you ill?"

"No."

"Faint from hunger. We haven't eaten."

"Partly." She straightened up. "My knees gave way from relief most of all."

"I know what you mean. The enemy you know is better than the one who hides in fog and shadows. But no more walking for you! We'll spend Master Tangorn's fee on a meal and a carriage to take us back to the palace."

"You're thinking," she said.

We sat in a hired carriage, the most comfortable and expensive I could find; the horses were beautiful matched bay mares and the driver on the seat well before us wore spotless black livery.

"I did so all the while you were being examined. Now I'm putting pieces of a puzzle together. Tell me: what do Queen Thaliara and Queen Elowar have in common?"

"Both women. Both rulers."

I tsk-tsked her.

"Both are beholden in some way to King Jehan of Hiaraniard."

"Closer. Now go a step further. Something strange."

"Strange? The strangest thing we know of Elowar is her sudden youth."

"Yes."

"But Thaliara—wait a moment." She frowned, remembering. "That boy said, 'They say that she is still as young and beautiful as when she was taken.' "

"Yes."

"Kin, that's meaningless. She was beautiful at seventeen, she is beautiful at thirty; observers have noted it. So what?"

"It may mean nothing, but it bothers me. Some men, adoring the flush of youth, like their women at seventeen. Some men, appreciating the ripening of beauty, prefer their women at thirty."

"So?"

"Would a man who preferred women of seventeen say that about Thaliara at thirty?"

"Probably not."

"Would a man who preferred women of thirty not say, 'She is *more* beautiful than she was when she was taken.'?"

"Yes. Especially a courtier. But Kin, I think you're reading far more into the remark of a boy who's never seen her than is warranted."

"I'd agree with you. Except for Queen Elowar and what we've seen of her. Halleyne, I have to go with her."

"To Mount Rozinki."

"Yes. To find out what is happening. To learn what King Jehan has in store for both our countries. If Elowar's party has already departed, I'll get a fast horse and follow."

"I think that would be a mistake. They'd want you dead, especially Sheroit and Teuper. They will try to silence you."

"I'll have to keep a step ahead of them."

"Then we'll go. Arrange for us to join the queen's party or follow it."

"You're not going, Halleyne. You're with child."

She gave me a level look. It was not a friendly one. "Did you just try to issue me an order?"

"No. An irrefutable argument."

"I refute it. The queen travels in a coach as comfortable as this one. So do her ladies-in-waiting, most of whom are far more delicate than I, even now."

"Even so, the Western Trade Route is a rough road, and everything but horses and goat-carts will be abandoned when we reach the mountains. Halleyne, you risk our son's life if you go."

She turned away for a long moment. When she looked at me again, her face was pale and hard, like alabaster. "Yes, I do. I could lose him. And if I do, I will mourn him . . . and live with the sorrow. I'm certain it will linger even with the next child we have together. But if I stay behind, and lose *you*, and have to wonder for the rest of my life if you would have survived had I been there . . . that is a sorrow I don't think I could live with."

"Halleyne—"

"Kin, don't ever put me from you unless you mean for it to be forever."

I glared at her in silence for long moments. "Well, you have given me what I could not give you."

"An order?"

"An irrefutable argument."

Chapter Eight

We were over most of our irritation with one another by the time we dismissed the coach before the palace walls.

Inside the walls, everything was a storm of activity. The great plaza before the palace proper was heavy with traffic and with the activities of men, women, horses, and coaches, a fury of saddling and sack-packing and good-bye-waving and list-checking. I counted around sixty travelers, among them about thirty guards—about right for a queen's cross-country trek through secure territory. I imagined the queen would be picking up more guards at Samaithe, just before crossing the Liedan border into mountain lands.

"Hold a moment," I told Halleyne, "and I'll make sure we have a place on this caravan."

I hurried over to where I saw the queen standing. She was surrounded by functionaries. As I got closer, I had what should not have been a surprise: she was in rider's gear. She'd been an avid horsewoman in her youth but had stopped making longer treks on horseback many years ago.

Her brow arched as she saw me approach. "Kin. I'd wondered where you were."

126

"Out shopping, Majesty. Buying my lady a mirror, feeding her, braining rival suitors who pursued her too closely, that sort of thing. Could I have a word with you in private?"

She gave a little shooing gesture and those around her withdrew to a discreet distance. I was pleased; this instant acquiescence on her part meant either she held me in some regard or was very curious about what I had to say. The major-domo, the one of them with the longest list in hand, was not so pleased; he shot me an annoyed glance.

"My wife and I would most enjoy accompanying you on your journey and think we could be of help to you thereon."

"In what way?"

"We know some of your secrets, and wish to help protect them for you."

She laughed. "What secrets?"

"Well, we know whom you will choose to be Jerno's successor."

"You do not."

"His successor will be the next child born of you."

Her smile faded. "A cruel joke. It is well known I am past childbearing years." But her tone was not that of a hurt woman. There was challenge in it.

"You were when I left with the king. But now you are not. You are young and vital. And freshly divorced. Were I not recently wed and very happily matched, I'd take a charge at you myself."

Her face took on an expression of amusement and mock outrage. "You are quite a different Kin Underbridge than the one who served Jerno as valet. It's very becoming. But I know from Zilona's tale that you have no love for Sheroit dar Bontine. You cannot rid yourself of the thought that it was the true Sheroit shipwrecked with you, can you? He will be there. I cannot bring into his presence a dangerous man who hates him. It would be very embarrassing to have you murder him during the wedding, Kin. Or murder King Jehan."

Another piece fell into place. "I will not move against King Jehan unless I have proof of his guilt, proof that you yourself will accept. And I will not move against Sheroit at all; I will abandon revenge against him. Because he was, after all, only obeying the will of his ruler, Jehan . . . and we all have made poor choices in such obedience. Is Sheroit not the one who courts you, the man who may be the sire of Lieda's future ruler?"

"What makes you think so?"

"Oh, the timbre of your voice when you say his name . . . and the fact that you sought to protect him from me before you did the same for King Jehan, the man to whom you owe your new youth and strength. Clear sign you held him in very high . . . and personal . . . regard."

She gave me a narrow look, trying to divine what else I knew. It cheered me that the arrows of my guesses had struck to the center of the target two or three times in quick succession.

"Well, then," she said. "I would doubtless profit from your presence. Make ready soon. We leave before the sun is much lower."

I smiled and bowed, then returned to the side of my wife.

"And?" she asked.

"We have a place in the caravan. But I can't kill Sheroit any more."

"You sadden me."

"Be of good cheer; I won't have to kill him. When we're done, half the world will want him dead."

"The queen certainly looked amused."

"I flirted with her."

She gave me a look of mock horror. "Before my very eyes!"

"Darling, I would never flirt so behind your back."

We entered our quarters to begin packing. We'd taken no more than two steps from the door when they came at us from the shadows, two men with swords out, charging from opposite sides.

As my opponent brought his sword up for his first stroke I lunged at him, went under his blow; I felt his forearm crack down atop my shoulder as I bore him to the floor. I was able to draw my sleeve-knife; as he reached for it with his free hand, too slow, I struck into his neck.

Then I, too slow, rolled off his dying form, rose, lurched toward my wife in the cold, anguished, despairing knowledge that I could do no more than avenge her—

Her attacker was on the floor. The rug I'd placed there was wrapped atop him. My wife, her expression desperate, was atop that, clinging to the attacker, keeping him blind. She'd done to him what I'd done to the guards that very morning, pulled the rug out from under him.

He flailed about and she fell free. As he got the rug off him I grabbed his head and pulled it back, exposing his neck. I put the edge of my knife to it. He was a young man, black-bearded, in good form. He looked at me with fear dawning in his eyes.

Halleyne sat up. She looked frightened but unhurt.

I told the man, "Give me correct answers and you can live. Who sent you here to kill us?"

He swallowed. "Minister Gastin."

"Why?"

"I don't know."

"Did you just try to kill my wife?"

He looked confused, swallowed again. "Minister Gastin ordered—"

"That's a 'yes.' Wrong answer." With a sudden, savage motion I cut his throat. He jerked, clutching at the wound, as a spray of blood spurted up past me and danced across the ceiling. I felt some of it fall on me like rain. Then the would-be assassin fell over.

Halleyne stood without my help and came into my arms. "Are you hurt?"

"No. Just scared. Why would the Minister of Trade want us dead?"

"We knew King Jehan had to have well-placed confederates on both courts. If Gastin is one, then he's just cleaning up for his master, ridding himself of Landfall's survivors—"

"The king—"

It was not far to the suite where Jerno and Viriat had been installed. When we reached it, there were guards outside; nearly twice the usual contingent, in fact, and many wore the uniforms of city guards rather than the more stylish uniforms of the palace guard.

They came alert as they saw me, blood-spattered and menacing of expression, approaching them. The officer on duty still saluted. "Judge Underbridge."

I barged up to him, for he stood just before the door. "Open up. The king may be in danger."

"The king has ordered no disturbances. He is in conference with Minister Gastin—"

The officer made a strangled noise then as Halleyne, who had crept up beside him, grabbed the lower hem of his cloak and gave it a ferocious yank, pulling him off-balance and choking him. How easily some forget that with the right blade or the right leverage the tiniest of people can be dangerous. Before his fellows could react I seized the door-handle and threw it open, banging it into the face of the officer's partner.

Within, in the center of the king's antechamber, stood Minister Gastin.

He was a tall old man, a decade senior to my father, with wispy white hair and cheery brown eyes. In weight he was much closer to Halleyne than to me.

He stood with Viriat's neck in one hand, King Jerno's in the other, and held them both above the ground, strangling them. Their faces were blue and purple, their kicks against him ineffectual. He looked a little startled as I entered.

I heard steel rasp and weapons clash behind me. The minister's guards had to be falling on the king's.

Gastin's eyes flickered as he considered. I tried to think as he must be thinking. And when he hurled Viriat at me, easily as a man might hurl a ripe fruit at an offensive minstrel, I anticipated the move and stepped aside. I got my knife into my hand again and charged him.

He struck me with the king. Jerno's massive weight hammered me to the side, slamming me to the floor. But the blow also tore Jerno free from the minister's grip; the king fell beside me.

"Damn you, Kin," the minister said, his voice almost pleasant, as I struggled, dazed, to stand up. "You've certainly fouled the waters here. If I don't kill all of you, I'll have to make a run for it. Inconvenient." He stalked toward us, a wizened, minuscule figure of menace.

Viriat was on his feet, and the one-time bodyguard wasted no time. He hefted one of the chamber's well-stuffed chairs, charged forward, and brought it down atop the minister.

For all his unnatural strength, Gastin weighed no more than he had before, had no greater sense of balance. He fell over, the chair atop him.

A guard stumbled into the room, bloody, trying to make sense of what he saw. Viriat tore the pole-axe from his fingers, and swung it at the chair and Gastin.

Gastin threw the chair off. I heard it smash into the far wall of the chamber. Then the edge of the axe hit him right over the heart, cracking ribs. Gastin screamed.

Viriat whirled the weapon around into a spearman's grip and thrust. The pole-axe's spear point took the minister in the side and crunched through lung and heart. Gastin screamed once more and died.

Viriat and I joined the guards in the hall, but that fight was almost done. Gastin's guards, forced into action after losing the advantage of surprise, were cut down or imprisoned to a man. Halleyne was unhurt. I directed the king's guards to drag the prisoners inside. We made sure the door was bolted.

The king's face was fading from blue to an angry red. His voice was raspy and harsh. "Kin, what in all the hells was this about?"

I nodded to Gastin. "I don't know how long it's been, but Gastin is King Jehan's man. Years ago, he guaranteed that another royal heir would die, clearing the way for Thaliara, by persuading you to impale Queen Lia's niece. He may have tried to clear the way for Buyan, too—perhaps it was he who convinced your son Tarno to kill himself to get your attention. And he isn't alone; it may be that many of the nobles who supported Elowar's strange decisions are also Jehan's men."

Gastin's body twitched. There were gasps from the guards; we all drew back.

His arms and legs twitched randomly. It could have been dying spasms, but I would have sworn the man was already dead. It looked for all the world like the motions of something inside Gastin trying to get out. Then he was still again.

"Kin, go tell the queen. Bring her here."

"A bad idea, Majesty. She is about to leave on her trip to Mount Rozinki; notifying her would only complicate matters, delaying them. Halleyne and I will be accompanying her. We will try to keep her safe; perhaps keeping Gastin's treachery secret is something we can use to bargain for more knowledge."

Jerno swore but nodded. He pointed to the guard-captain. "You! To whom do you owe your loyalty, the queen or me?"

The officer winced. "To the reigning ruler, Majesty. For now, to the queen. When you are confirmed, to you."

"Fair enough. I charge you with cleaning this all up. Keeping it secret. Rooting out every little bit of Gastin's treachery. You will obey all my commands in this, except where they directly contradict the queen's."

"Yes, Majesty."

Jerno, Viriat, Halleyne, and I retreated to the king's bed-chamber. We told them of the assassins in our room, of what we'd done to get Zilona rescued. The king promised to pretend, for now, that Zilona was his mistress and to give her rescuer a reward appropriate to the rescue of a royal favorite.

"As soon as the crown is on my head," he said, "I will send a new ambassador, one loyal to me, to Mount Rozinki. He will be under orders to give you whatever help you ask for. I may be obliged to honor Elowar's treaties, but I'm not obliged to cooperate with assassination attempts. If Jehan is responsible, I will bring him to ruin."

We were later than I wanted to be returning to the queen's caravan. After all, we had to pack, to change into unbloodied clothes, and to settle our nerves. We endured the queen's chiding with good grace, smiling as though we were not bruised and unnerved.

I was given a big bay gelding named Willow—so-named for the reedy thinness of his legs when he was a colt. He was a gentle mount, chosen by some wag, I think, to embarrass me, for he wasn't a real "warrior's horse," but after years out of the saddle and the way I'd been battered by King Jerno's hurtling body I was happy to have a good-tempered, steady mount.

Halleyne was placed on the coach of ladies-in-waiting; the queen had brought a bare-minimum four ladies along, so there was sufficient room to accommodate another. Halleyne had them laughing to tales of Queen Lia and listening avidly to stories of our shipwreck well before we were outside the boundaries of Bekalli.

I was interested to find out that the military officer in charge of the guards was General Oakwall; he waved and smiled at me as he mounted his horse and then ignored me for most of the duration of the trip. His presence suggested that it was not he who had rescued Zilona; the rescuer would surely want to remain in Bekalli, the better to hand over the girl to King Jerno personally and receive his reward immediately.

Westward we traveled along the coast road, a fine highway that afforded us good breezes and beautiful clifftop vistas of the seas north of Feyndala. The view and cheerful companions settled our nerves but did not, alas, diminish the amount of dust we ate; traveling alone on these roads was bad enough, but to be in the middle of a caravan was far worse.

In the morning of the fourth day out, I awoke snuggled against my wife in the tiny inn room we had taken—barely the size of a pantry—and Halleyne, already awake, said "The spirits are here."

"Which?"

"The ones I felt before. At the palace."

"The ones that scream in silence." I slid my hand

atop her abdomen, as though I could feel our child growing beneath. "Do you think they are following us?" Perhaps, I did not add, to invade and take up residence in our child?

"I think they are carried around like cargo. Last night I sung to keep spirits away from me, and from the baby. And I could feel them, some distance away but still near, repelled by my song but held in place. Unable to escape or protest the affront my song was to them."

"Spirits who are like cargo. What sort of song would Shallia make of that?"

But that put us in mind of Shallia, and the fact that her nighttime spirit had, with her magic, not yet found Halleyne again. It had now been thirty days since we had left Fishtail Island, and I prayed that Snake-Mother had stayed asleep all that time and would sleep still longer.

On the days to come I kept my eyes open for the way this expedition's carriers and servants handled their cargo. Was any parcel or trunk carried with more delicacy? Did any of the nobles become agitated when a package was moved?

No. I grew irritated. Whomever was carting those spirits around was treating them like common baggage. But Halleyne sang her "Spring Hunting Song" and felt their presence every night from then on.

Ten days out of Bekalli, where the road diverged from the coast, we left the road and turned southwest along older, more rutted dirt tracks used by farmers to bring their crops to the coastal cities. It was an easy ride for me, but I winced to see the way the ladies' coach was bounced around. Halleyne took it all in good stride and I did not see her health or temper begin to fail. It was, I know, too soon to really worry that a jounce could harm either her or our son, but knowing not to worry and not worrying are as different as the idea of the mule and the mule: the idea of the mule is both useful and reasonable, while the mule has a mind of its own and goes where it will.

On this stretch of the road, surrounded by bare furrowed fields, there were few towns and no inns. At the end of each traveling day, we would sweep onto the closest farm and startle the family living there almost to death; Burslan, the queen's court magician, would make an assault on the barn, using his arts to banish cattle ticks and other vermin as well as odors that might offend the noses of the highborn. General Oakwall would arrange for the slaughter and roasting of the tastiest-looking livestock, and we would dine well into the night.

But Elowar did not choose to earn the ill will of the minor lords and major cottswolders we'd so invaded. She did things, as her husband had, with an eye toward maintaining among the visited people some idea that they had been honored by her presence. So upon our departure the next morning one of us always gave the farmer a good handful of coins to compensate him for his losses. Jerno's grandfather had nearly been dethroned by angry nobles who'd been beggared by the costs of supporting his traveling court (the revolt might have succeeded, had they enough money to hire good troops); the current king and queen had learned from this.

After nearly ten days of travel in this way, our

rutted dirt track finally met the Western Trade Route. This road was dirt in some stretches, hardpack clay over stone in others, with royal engineers working at places along its length to turn the one into the other. Within a few years it would be a true highway stretching from Soort's Hill to Samaithe and the mountains beyond. At one point on our journey, as we crossed over a wide-flowing stream, I was able to trot up beside the ladies' coach and tell my wife, "I helped build this very bridge when I was companion to Prince Balaquin."

"Ha! Knowing you, you probably convinced the stones to assemble themselves while you lay about napping."

"Don't tell your new friends all my secrets, dear."

Back on this more civilized road, we were able to spend more nights than not in town inns and the residences of local mayors and governors, though a few nights were still played out before the startled eyes of farmers and, increasingly, cattle ranchers.

In most of these places, rumor had preceded us that King Jerno had returned. Message-riders and fast-moving traders must have carried the rumor with them the very day we left Bekalli and preceded us. But there was no hint of the story that Elowar was stepping down as queen; that told me that she chose her personal guards for their loyalty and discretion and that she had not chosen to noise that particular piece of news about. By now she was probably princess, not queen, but the news of Jerno's resumption of the throne would be following us days behind.

Exactly thirty days after we departed Bekalli, as the land was becoming increasingly rolling, we topped a hill and looked down on Samaithe.

She was a city built on trade in proximity to Lieda's greatest enemy. She lay at the crossroads of the two trade roads that were later named Knights' Road and the Western Trade Route, at the edge of the foothills of the mountains lying between Lieda and Terosalle. A well-walled city built where underground springs emerged, she was known for the quality of her baths. Outside the city proper were many other enclosures, where walls protected a few buildings and large open spaces. These were private caravanserai, where merchant caravans could rest one day or several within the safety the walls represented.

Before dark we entered the city gates, and within a few minutes more were dismounting before the regional governor's mansion.

All except for me. I extended a hand down for my wife and pulled her up to sit before me.

"You're not joining us, Kin?" asked the queen.

"I'd not willingly abandon your company for anything, Majesty," I told her. "But I've a sister living here, and family duty compels me to visit."

"The trader Brightpool's wife, isn't she?"

"She is."

"My regards to her and her husband."

After a few minutes of seeking directions from people on the city's well-finished streets, we dismounted before the Brightpool estate as a servant took my horse's reigns.

I whistled. I'd never visited here before, and while Fara's letters made it evident that she and her husband never suffered from want, it was now clear to me that understatement was among her skills.

The house was built in Terosai style, nearly windowless, almost featureless on the outside. But it was huge, some hundred paces long along its front facing, made of finely dressed stone.

Another servant conducted us through the main doors, along a long, sinisterly dark corridor that—if Terosai architecture was truly being followed—must feature unseen arrow-slits and hidden points of observation.

And then we reached the third well-known trait of Terosai design, the central court. Some such courts were open to the sky, some roofed; my sister's was a happy blend of both, for I could see that the roof above was equipped with gears and mechanisms by which its center section might be drawn open like a sliding door.

This was a two-story court, a garden with a bubbling fountain, marble benches, and flower beds; the columns held up a balcony level. And it was from there, behind us as we emerged into the court, that I was hailed: "Kin!"

We turned. Above us on the balcony was Fara—a much-changed Fara, from the last time I'd seen her.

She was *tall*. A final summer of growth must have had its way with her since the last time I saw her, years ago. She was now the height of my father.

She was elegant. No longer the rangy tomboy, she was attired in a flowing gown of silk dyed in glorious southern pastels, her long hair flowing and unbound instead of done up in a practical braid, her even features now bearing a stamp of sophistication.

She was heavy with child, unable to lean over the railing as she stared down at me.

And, instead of exhibiting joy as my parents had at my return from the dead, she was suspicious. This was clear from her stiff posture, the narrowing of her eyes.

"Fara!" I cried. "You are with child. Either Edan is not as hopeless as I'd feared, or your taste in men has broadened since your wedding."

"Wretch," she said, "why do I have a white scar on my knee?"

"What?"

"Tell me! Word for moons has it that there are double-spirits abroad. The real Kin can tell me why I bear a scar. A double-spirit can only play target for my archers." She gestured and I turned. Opposite her on the far balcony waited a pair of long-bowmen, mountain archers by the look of them; they had arrows nocked but not drawn and did not look as though they wanted to become my friends.

"Ah," I said, and turned back to her. "Well. Not to put too fine a point on it, you have a scar because you are noisy, slow, and stupid."

"Liar!"

"Noisy because as we explored the attic you could not help but knock boxes from atop one another and send them crashing to the floor."

"Filthy liar!"

"Slow because you could not get to the hatch leading to the servants' hall before Father came up to investigate, and had to dive for it, and tore your flesh open getting through."

"Stinking liar!"

"And stupid because you were up there with me in the first place."

Her expression changed to a smile, almost beatific. "Kin! It *is* you." She drew back from the rail and tottered down a nearby stairwell at a rate that was entirely inappropriate for her condition. Then she threw herself into my arms. "How did you survive? How are you here? Do Mother and Father know? Who's this?"

"Fara Brightpool, I present Halleyne, special emissary of the government-in-exile of Queen Lia of Terosalle . . . and my wife."

She embraced Halleyne. "You are welcome in my house, sister." She turned back to me. "Wrench and wrench?" she asked, brightly.

Code-words of the Underbridge siblings. I felt a moment of regret that there were now only two of us alive to understand them. "Yes, her arms were wrenched before she'd represent the queen in this way. And no, I didn't wrench her arms to make her marry me. Are you going to feed us or not?"

Over dinner, held in the lesser dining hall, which she'd decorated with heavy wood planking and furniture like Father's hall back home, I told her the whole story, including the difficulties surrounding the conception of our child and the danger he faced.

"So Jerno is to be king again," she said.

"He probably already is. Even as slowly as the Council of Judges might choose to work, he's probably had the crown on his head for two weeks or more."

"I'll have to move quickly. Edan is at Fairy Bridge settling trouble with his captains there, so it will be my task to profit as much as I can from the change in power."

"Placing bets," I said, "currying favor with the currently disgraced Jerno loyalists, that sort of thing."

"That very sort."

"But don't ever hint that Jerno is resuming his rank or Elowar is stepping down. If my reasoning is correct, that might prove fatal for her. Which may mean fatal for *us*."

"You've nothing to fear from me." She rose and moved to where a great map of Feyndala adorned the wall, much in the same place that a similar map decorated Father's hall. "You know, I can tell you almost to the day when this 'youthening' you say King Jehan is dispensing came about."

"Tell me."

"On this last Day of the Dead."

In both Lieda and Terosalle, we observed a holy day called Sirdam, last day of the calendar year, dedicated to the memories of our ancestors. A solemn day, a day of reflection. But the day itself was a reflection of an older celebration, the Day of the Dead, still observed by the mountain clans. The Day of the Dead lies between the last day of the old year—some ten days earlier than our last day—and the first day of the new year; it is a day that lies outside their calendar, seldom mentioned and never with cheer. The mountain folk believe that the spirits of their dead ancestors walk free that day, and any death or disappearance taking place then is attributed to vengeful ancestors.

"Why then?" Halleyne asked.

"It is the day Jehan won his long campaign. Come, look."

We joined her before the map.

She pointed to the Black Rock Reaches, the western peninsula where mountains jutted aggressively out into the sea, the western equivalent of Hanuman's Point. "See, here, this is the area where Jehan first appeared, in Year Twenty of Jerno's reign. He was suddenly just there, war-chief of the Black Rock Clan, and led them in many feuds and battles. Often against the Red Lances. I learned all this from Edan and his sire, for the mountain clan wars have considerable effect on land trade."

She gestured a little further inland and south to indicate Red Lance territory. "And then, in Year Two-and-Twenty, the Black Rock chief and the Red Lance chief died in battle with one another. The Black Rocks won that battle and drove the Red Lances into banditry. Jehan became chief of the Black Rocks and a bandit calling himself Cenpeydon became chief of the Red Lances."

I snorted. Cenpeydon was a word in the old form of the Liedan language; it meant "High King" and was sometimes trotted out to describe King Jerno. "That was the same year the war started."

"Oh, yes. And the same year Edan began sending me gift after gift."

"Cheeky runt. He should have waited until you were sixteen at least. How does this all get us to the Day of the Dead?"

"Well, for years, Jehan and his Black Rock clan fought against the other mountain clans. He beat some, destroyed some, absorbed some, extended his territory almost as far as the Western Trade Route. But it was slow, hard going against stubborn enemies.

"And then late last year he invited all the chiefs he hadn't conquered to come visit him in neutral territory—the northern mountains of the Route, where Liedan forces kept things in order. They had a grand conclave of the clans on the last days of their year . . . and on their Day of the Dead, the day that doesn't happen, thirteen chiefs of the mountain clans swore him allegiance. In the days to follow, more did. All with no further battle."

"But the Red Lances didn't," Halleyne said.

"You are correct."

"And he attacked them, and defeated them, and freed Captain Buyan and Princess Thaliara."

"Again, correct. And oh, the stories that have come from that battle." Fara looked revolted instead of pleased. "Chief Jehan and Chief Cenpeydon battling in personal combat on the support arch the engineers had put in at Mount Preskon. In full view of both armies. With greatswords. Cenpeydon admitting with great glee to capturing both Buyan and Thaliara in order to start the war, and keeping it going to destroy both nations. All until Jehan cut him down and kicked him off the arch. Kin, can you remember how you used to get in trouble for spattering minstrels with rotten fruit for singing of Thaliara's glories? I'm of a mind to hire brats like you to do the same to the ones now singing of Jehan."

"Off the arch," Halleyne said.

"Yes."

"So he was dashed to pieces below."

"Yes."

"I'll wager a dozen royal crowns that his face was battered beyond recognition."

I felt obliged to interrupt. "Darling, I don't have a dozen royal crowns."

"I do."

"Where'd you get them?"

Fara said, "Hush, brat. Your wife would win were I stupid enough to accept the bet. Yes, he was as 'ruined as though the gods themselves had betrod his face,' or so the latest lamentable lay expresses it."

"And these chiefs," Halleyne said. "The ones who swore loyalty."

"They're 'barons' now. That's a Suinomen noble rank."

"Yes, and Rozinki, which he's named his citadel for, is the Suinomen capital. I know my maps, too. It's evident Jehan is an adventurer or exile from there. What I was going to ask is this: do any of these chiefs exhibit new youth and vigor?"

Fara considered it and then nodded. "Oh, not youth specifically. But old Benefor Skullcrack, chief—I mean baron—of the Highrock Clan, just fought in the clan's chief-choosing battle. They do that once every twelve years to decide who leads them. He won last time, barely, and was five-and-fifty then, so it was well-known that he would fall or quit the field this time to become counselor to the new chief."

"But he won instead," I said.

"Handily. Splitting his cousin's skull just to earn his nickname again." She looked between us. "Kin, I wish you would not go into Hiaraniard."

I smiled. "I do too."

"You could stay here. In war or peace, Samaithe is much the same, well away from the action. If men seek you, I can hide you; if they do not seek you, I can show you off. You and Halleyne could both be counselors to the governor and earn a fat purse every year."

"All true," I said. "But these connivers' actions have cost us two brothers, so I have revenge to think about. And Queen Elowar rides into their midst, and I still have regard for her in spite of her recent fit of anger, so I have her safety to think about. And Sheroit is still out there, and may plan to silence me or Halleyne now or in the future, so I have our lives to think about. All of these reasons scream at me to enter Hiaraniard."

Chapter Nine

"I'm awake." I heard Halleyne say this and it roused me from sleep. I opened my eyes.

Hers were still closed in sleep. And a woman's hand, not entirely opaque, tried tenderly but futilely to brush some of her straying hair from her face.

I held my breath and rolled over to see. It was Shallia again, not aware of me, concentrating hard on my lady. She stood in the center of the bed from the thighs up, as though it were as insubstantial as she.

Shallia spoke. I heard only a few words, disconnected phrases. Halleyne truly awoke in the middle of it and stared wonderingly at the image of her friend. When Shallia was through speaking, Halleyne said, "Gods' luck to you."

And Shallia was gone like smoke carried away by a winter wind.

"What news?" I asked.

She gave me a glowing smile. "Good news. *Driftwood* has arrived. And though Snake-Mother is nearly awake, she is not truly awake."

"Thank the gods. They'll be out of there in a day."

Halleyne gave out a happy sigh and relaxed, her eyes closing. She said something indistinct and was almost instantly asleep.

Too early by far the next morning, Halleyne and I rose and bid my sister good-bye.

That took a while. She loaded us down with gifts she must have been assembling half the night. Clothes as befitted a judge of Lieda and a *thalahai* of Terosalle, knives aplenty (she, like me, had inherited my father's love of the things), pouches of money ("One Liedan, one Terosai, one Hiaraniard—you never know *whom* you'll have to bribe, and I'd give you Bontiniard coin as well if they had yet minted any."), names of trade contacts she had with the mountain clansmen, a good broadsword of Naisley make and a set of good chain mail for me, jewels, and a picnic basket. When we finally got through the thank-yous and embraces and kisses and tears to mount up, Willow was a heavily-loaded horse. Fortunately, when we rejoined the royal party before the governor's mansion, Halleyne took the picnic basket and most of our sudden wealth aboard the coach with her.

Now we were a much larger party, our guards having grown in number from thirty to a hundred and thirty. Our additions were a detachment of the Samaithe High Banners, the same cavalry unit I'd fetched in my futile effort to reach Prince Balaquin in time. I knew them to be hard-riding, tireless soldiers; Queen Elowar could be in no better hands. Among the hundred who joined us were eleven women, many of them of mixed descent, Liedan and mountain-clan, and most of those rode the hairy mountain horses that could climb hillsides with almost the skill of goats.

And speaking of goats, gone were the delicate royal carriages perched atop ingenious leaf-springs that absorbed many of the jarring shocks of ordinary road travel. Gone too were the horses that drew them. In their place were Fadornal goats, bred centuries ago by mountain men with, it is said, the help of mountain mages. Fadornal goats are the size of ponies, a little mean and quite bad-smelling, but sure-footed beyond belief on treacherous mountain tracks. They drew low, rugged carts heaped with hay covered with thick linen; these carts had to serve the ladies-in-waiting in place of the fine coaches.

Immediately south of Samaithe the land began to rise and the road became rocky and serpentine. Though previously I'd spent some time each day riding alongside the queen or among the cavalry officers, I now forsook their company to place myself behind my wife's coach at all times. In three days we were at the mouth of the first of the mountain valley passes, and after three more days we were spending cold, cold nights in the higher climes.

Soon after, in spite of clever tricks with the way she arrayed her garments, Halleyne's condition was recognized and then widely announced by one of the ladies-in-waiting. I received back-pounding congratulations from General Oakwall and most of the cavalry officers.

But nothing of the sort from the queen. She took me aside. "Kin, are you an idiot?"

I managed a fair approximation of her voice and delivery. "'For only an idiot would have brought his pregnant wife on a dangerous mountain trek—'"

"You can't dismiss my thoughts by mocking them."

"No, I can't. But I can say this. I could only stop her from coming by divorcing her and then locking her up. You've been divorced without your leave; I've been made a prisoner without my leave; I don't think either of us would wish these fates on Halleyne."

"Well . . . perhaps not."

As we walked back to the night's place of encampment, a broadening in the stony gash that could only approximately be termed a mountain pass, I said, "Would you like to take Sheroit's true measure?"

"You're talking against him again."

"Not at all. I'm just inviting you to gauge him."

"What do you suggest?"

"Don't tell him immediately that you are no longer Queen of Lieda. Let him know that you locked Jerno up when he was found but not that he was released soon after you departed. Then, later, tell him of your abdication."

She was silent for a few moments, but slapped her riding crop into her hand several times. "You think he will love me less because I have no great kingdom for the both of us to rule."

"I do. I also think he is canny enough that it will take him mere moments to conceal that fact. You will have to watch and listen, during the first moments after you tell him, for the strain in his voice, the grimace he tries to turn into a smile. Those few moments are the truth of his feeling for you, Princess."

"I do not care for your meddling, Kin."

"Who does? But I am sure you long to know the truth. This is a way of finding one part of it."

She left me as we rejoined the camp and did not speak to me for a couple of days thereafter.

Though Halleyne and I knew disquiet as we came closer and closer to the citadel of King Jehan, we could find some solace in the beauty of our surroundings. The Feyndalan mountains were jutting marvels, greater in size and more magnificent in beauty than anything the engineers of our two kingdoms would ever build. They were carpeted in green on their lower reaches, graduating, as they lay in shadow, through rich blues and purples the likes of which no ocean had ever seen, to whiteness at their peaks, for winter never left the tallest mountains. In the mornings, fog muted the colors and added a drama of depth to our surroundings, and I felt I was seeing dioramas made by the master craftsmen of the gods.

Of course, all this appreciation fled whenever some icy wind came roaring off one of those peaks and ripped through us, carrying away heat we dressed so carefully to preserve, sometimes causing horses to stumble or carts to totter.

On two nights we were able to sleep within walls, inside strategic fortresses built along the Trail. One of these, Fort Lavvan, the more northern, was small, a deterrent once thought adequate to prevent Terosai invasion, but soon after Prince Balaquin's death we learned that the Terosai had learned a way to circumvent it with a force on foot. The other, newer one, Highpeak Citadel, several days further south, was at the narrowest part of the highest pass on the route, making it a welcome sight for cold travelers such as ourselves but not a welcome assignment for an army man of Lieda.

Past that, it was several more days before we sighted the riverbed that was the entrance to the alternate southern route. It had no name in the days when Prince Balaquin and I worked to commence a fortress, but now, General Oakwall said, it was called the Black Rock Road. Here and there, I could see signs of new building along its length, where mountain men had put up wooden bridges of fair sophistication over difficult river crossings or had widened the road by cutting or shattering stone.

One night, as we slept under star-filled skies, I was awakened by a cry of alarm from one of the posted guards. Half the camp roused at the sound and called for an explanation.

"It was there!" cried the young guard, pointing straight at me and Halleyne. "A woman, a faint figure prowling among us."

I looked into Halleyne's eyes. She nodded. Shallia had been here.

"Was she pretty?" I asked the guard.

"Yes, sir!"

"Was she dressed for this weather?"

"No, sir."

"Then she wasn't real, was she? Son, when we get back to Samaithe, you need to find yourself a woman."

Half the camp laughed at the guard's expense. Only General Oakwall roused. I was sure he was going to give the boy a talking-to for falling asleep, having provocative dreams on duty, and awakening people in the dead of night.

"What did she say?" I asked in a whisper.

"I didn't understand it all. She's scared. She was infected with Snake-Mother's little serpent-spirits for a time. *Driftwood* didn't depart Fishtail Island. She said Byriver showed up. I don't understand. Jerno Byriver should still be in Bekalli. I got the impression she meant a ship."

"There's a ship of the line named *Byriver*. Named for the king, of course. Elowar might have dispatched it to Landfall to get the survivors. That sounds like her sense of humor at work. But why aren't they off the island yet?"

"I don't know." She shivered in my arms. "There's more. Confusion. A mad thing among them. I just didn't understand."

"It will be all right," I told her, and prayed it wasn't a lie.

And finally there was the Citadel at Mount Rozinki.

The former Mount Preskon was a dual-peak mountain, with the cleft between the peaks the only passage suited for horses and carts in the entire area. Just above where the peaks diverged, the western mountain extended a great slab of granite toward the eastern, a stone spar that was not too severe a slope on top and constituted a bridge across nearly two-thirds of the gap between the peaks. Caves dotted the mountainside just where the spar began, and had been the well-defended homes of bandit clans in centuries past.

Balaquin's idea had been to build a fort on that slab and extend an ambitious arch from the eastern peak to meet the stone spar. This would change it from a partial bridge to a complete bridge, making it easier to send troops down against the road from two directions. Such a fort would be extremely difficult to take. We had begun construction of the support arch when the elite Terosai force I mentioned came across us.

After that failed Terosai assault, work resumed on the fortress. I was not there to witness it, having been assigned as companion to the next princely son, Tarno, though I knew the arch was eventually completed and some walls constructed. But the engineering crews building the thing were under constant harassment from Terosai forces and mountain men both, so they eventually withdrew and the fortress was built at Highpeak instead.

What I expected, when we made our way along a final mountain-slope trail to come within sight of the citadel, was an arch and part of a wall in finely-placed Liedan stonework supplemented by new palisade walls of mountain wood. That is not what we saw.

The stone arch from the eastern mountain was indeed complete, a beautiful curve like those supporting the aqueducts that brought water down from the mountains in arid central Lieda, dark stone matching the natural spar extending from the west.

Atop the spar was a completed circuit wall, heavy dressed stones rising some twelve paces in height from the level of the stone shelf on which it rested. The eastern part of the wall was thus half-a-dozen paces higher than the western. At each corner of the wall was a fortified tower capped by a steeply-peaked wooden roof designed to slough snowfalls. The wall did not continue out atop the constructed arch. I could see no sign that the newer construction was inferior to the older.

Atop the walls were banners, colorfully heraldic, showing rampant animals and checked color-patterns—at least one, I guessed, for every clan that had sworn allegiance to Jehan. Beyond them rose the peaks of buildings—wooden, but evidently well-made, and three or four stories in height for me to be able to see their roofs.

Below, where the roadway passed through the cleft between the peaks, were tents and picket lines and other sign of encampment—or encampments. The tents were grouped in clusters, one large group of gaily-colored tents flying Terosai banners, other pockets of cruder cloth or leather tents flying the banners of mountain clans. I counted some seventy tents in all. There were men and some women among the tents, ranging in dress from brightly-clad courtiers to mountain riders, and many watched as we approached.

Then something detached itself from the under-side of the archway, just where it met the natural stone of the spar. It was a wooden box, perhaps five paces by five, and as high as my waist, with a wooden railing along the edge; at each corner was a set of ropes or cables. Standing within the box was a young woman in rich courtier's clothes. Her skirt and underblouse were a relatively subdued purple, but her vest, belt, and cap were a more festive violet, and the cap was decorated by a yellow feather as long as some sword blades; it twitched and shimmered with every move of the woman's head—or of the descending box. For try as the unseen controllers overhead might to make sure the thing descended in a steady, level manner, wind-gusts made it sway more and more as it came closer to the ground.

It touched down when we were still a hundred paces away. She of the magnificent feather emerged—for at one point the side wall and rail of the box was interrupted by a low door. She was handed the reins of a shaggy mountain horse by a soldier standing by; she mounted and came trotting up to us directly.

"It's Sora," said Elowar.

"You know her?" I asked.

"She's the new ruler of the Red Lances Clan—what's left of it—appointed so by King Jehan. She visited me in Bekalli a moon after the Black Rocks destroyed the Red Lances."

As Sora got nearer, I could see she was a beauty, and far younger than I had supposed; she was fifteen if a day. Her hair, worn long, was a brown the color of lacquered oak; her features were even and pixielike . . . and reminded me of someone. I could not place where I thought I'd seen her like before.

Sora called, "Majesty!" and came trotting up. She continued in mountain-accented but accomplished Liedan, "Hiaraniard welcomes its sister, mighty Lieda. I speak for King Jehan . . . but let me extend my own warm greetings to Her Majesty, Elowar." Her smile was warm and seemed genuine.

I dropped back until I was beside Halleyne's cart and helped her up into the saddle before me. "She seems familiar to me," she whispered.

"And to me."

Elowar stared past the girl, looking at the box and the cables stretching up to the arch overhead. "You got it working," she said.

Sora brought her horse alongside the queen's and we continued on toward the box. "Indeed we did, Majesty. It's much faster than going up the approach trail—and far safer."

Elowar gave her a dubious look but chose not to question this assertion. "Your king is away from his citadel?" she asked.

"No, he is present, but tied to his throne. He sends his regrets. He is caught up in matters of policy and rule and so could not meet you upon your arrival." Sora sounded very apologetic and comforting. She was very well-spoken for one so young, but I recalled that my sister Fara had been much the same.

"I regret he is so caught up in protocol," Elowar said. Her voice had become more than a little cool, and I didn't wonder why; for Jehan not to greet the party carrying Elowar's personal banner was either an insult between equals or a demonstration by one ruler of his superior place above another.

"Yes, Majesty, and he longs to greet you. Would you care to essay this most novel mechanism? It carries up to twenty with ease, or one horse and a smaller number of men."

Elowar gave her a cross look, indicating just what she thought of the idea of carting horses off into the sky, and pointed among her retinue to indicate who should come forward to be lifted in the first load. She chose two of her bodyguards, General Oakwall, the mage Burslan, the captain of the unit we'd taken on in Samaithe, two of the queen's ladies-in-waiting, her scribe . . . and me and Halleyne, the other two ranking members of her retinue. Our packs and boxes were carried up to be loaded onto the contraption.

We went "aboard" with some trepidation, some

of us standing around the edges and clutching the rails, the others standing in the middle and, I noted with amusement, clutching each other. Sora joined us and closed the little door, then made a rising-fist gesture toward the sky.

The slack in the cables was collected; they went taut. I thought, from the way they responded simultaneously and at precisely the same rate, that all four must have been attached to a single winch or other mechanism.

Then there was a great lurch and we were airborne—and swinging toward the eastern mountain face, for the box had been swinging toward the western when it had originally touched down. One of the soldiers swore and one of the ladies-in-waiting shrieked, but we were in no danger of striking the mountain face. Still, it felt to me that my stomach was left behind on that first swing and then took its own deliberate time in getting back to me.

As we rose, I was able to distinguish more details of the arrangement overhead. There was a hole in the construction where it met the mountain spar; it was a little larger than was needed to accommodate the box. As we came closer, I could see the mechanism of the winch above it, and heads peering down at us from the hole. When we were no more than five paces from it, the observers overhead extended down long wooden poles, which they used to guide the ropes so we were swung around to a specific orientation, making it possible to get the box up through a hole scarcely larger than it was.

Then we emerged into a large, barnlike building with the massive frame of the winch overhead.

Our box was raised a pace above the level of the
floor and stout beams were slid in under it; then
it was lowered to the beams. Sora opened the
door and two rough-looking men placed a gangplank before it.

And thus we came to the citadel of Mount
Rozinki.

Doors admitted us to the outside—atop the
well-made arch. I saw that it did have its own
low stone wall, doubtless to prevent the winds
from blowing some luckless visitor over the side
and to his doom. We stood before the citadel's
defensive wall; even should some force be able
to assault the citadel and seize control of the
winch, the fortress itself would still be secure.
The great gate in the center of the citadel wall
was open, and our too-familiar guide led us
through.

Within, the citadel was little different from other
forts. There were walls; just within were many
well-made buildings, barracks and kitchens and
workshops and the mansion residence of the king;
and at the center was the great courtyard where
military training could take place. I was intrigued
to see that the sloping surface of the mountain's
stone spar had been built up by piled dirt and
well-made retaining walls so it now fell away in
a series of terraces; the courtyard resembled
nothing so much as steps cut for giants. There
was plenty of foot traffic across it, soldiers moving
in and out of the barracks, kitchen staff carrying
trays of foods from the kitchens to the mansion,
armored soldiers training against one another with
wooden weapons.

And emerging from the mansion, the building

set against the western mountain slope—for no
stone wall was needed where nature had already
provided one—was Sheroit dar Bontine, the traitor
of the treaty expedition, who with Teuper dar
Hiaro and King Jehan had conspired to summon
many winds and smash our ships on the reefs of
the Landfall island. I felt my shoulders stiffen and
then was reminded by a tug on my arm that I
was crushing my wife's fingers. I tried to relax.

"This should be very interesting," Halleyne said.

The queen's whispered words floated back to
us—"Remember what you promised, Kin."

Then they were upon us. Sheroit, all dapper
beard and melodious voice, stooped to kiss the
queen's hand. "Majesty," said Sheroit, "you dazzle
like the sun—all about you fades to nothing, like
resentful night." Then his gaze fell upon me and
Halleyne and his expression turned to one of
absolute delight. "Kin! Lady Halleyne. So the story
is true. How delighted I am to see you well."
He took a glance at Halleyne's belly. "And pros-
pering."

I took his proffered hand. "I'm to understand
you have a story of your own. One in which you
and Teuper never even made it to the island we
visited."

"It's true; we were on an island prison all our
own. I'll give you all the particulars when you
have half a night to hear them." He looked
between us. "Is the other half of the tale true?
King Jerno yet lives?"

Elowar nodded. "He does. He is recuperating
at the Bekalli citadel. Under the care of very
attentive guards."

He looked at her, the very image of a lover

fearing painful news. "And the union between you—"

"Is done. In his absence, he also absented himself from our marriage."

"This must complicate your rule, Majesty."

"Certainly not." She stood a trifle taller. "He may have returned, but there is only one ruler over Lieda."

I tried not to slump in relief. She had decided to foster the story I'd suggested to her.

"Delighted to hear it; the alternative would have been a bitter reward for you. Come within, where we have warmth, and food, and entertainment. Oh, nothing like the court of Lieda has to offer, but King Jehan does well as he can . . ."

Into the very maw of our enemy, we followed the chattering negotiator.

As it turned out, we were not to be fed or entertained immediately. It was an hour or less until this night's court and dinner, so Sora summoned a servant to find a room for us, encouraging us to make ourselves ready and cheerful for the night's events.

It was, in truth, not much of a room. About half the size of the box we'd ridden into the sky, it might as well have been windowless, for the window opened out onto the face of the western mountain, a short stone's throw away. The bed was low, heavy furniture with a bare minimum of straw stuffed into a mattress. But all seemed clean, and the domestic mages had obviously kept it free of bedbugs and other parasites.

"We're obviously not high on their list of important personages," Halleyne said. "What do you have to be to warrant a chair and a closet?" She was in the midst of scrubbing off road-dust with a washrag and water from the basin on the table.

"Well, they don't yet know we're a judge and a *thalahai*. As soon as they know our current, probably ephemeral, titles, they'll gladly move our belongings into a much better-appointed room . . . so they can search them."

"Good point," she said. Finished, she began dressing in one of her finer garments, carefully chosen and stolen from the closet of the room we'd had in Bekalli; this one was a gown in dark blue. Over it she wrapped a golden chain Fara had given her, using it as a belt, and she added golden earrings. "Suitable?" she asked.

I continued scrubbing my ear and studied her. "You're a king's ransom in a blue velvet purse," I said.

She smiled, then composed herself where she sat. "I think, if these barbarous mountain men are as fond of ceremony as we civilized folk, that tonight's events may go well into the night."

"True."

"In which case I ought to do my day's rituals now instead of having to find some far less convenient time for them." She closed her eyes and took a steadying breath, then began singing the purgative notes that, combined with her native magical ability, would protect our baby from day to day.

She sang the sequence through a couple of times, her voice low and carefully modulated, then tilted her head, her eyes still closed, and began singing something else, her "Spring Hunting Song."

"Out spirit-hunting again?"

She nodded without interrupting her music.

Then her expression changed, became one of surprise and alarm. I dropped the washcloth and took up my short sword to stand beside her. Perhaps the steel would be of no use against whatever it was she felt . . . but I felt better for having it.

Her eyes opened and she stared past me at the door. I whirled.

Coming through the door was a man, if man he could be called. From the raven's-wings tattoos on his shoulders and his rough beard and hair, I'd say he was a mountain man. But he was gray—of skin as well as of hair and beard, a continuous tone like some grades of pretty building stone—and stark naked.

And when I say he was coming through the door, I do not mean that he was walking through an open doorway. The door stood closed and bolted as I'd left it. He oozed through it like a sticky jelly, parts of him clinging to the wood as he tried to pull free of it; more of him flowed into the room, especially by way of the gaps between the planks that made up the door. He gazed upon my wife with an expression of avarice. Or perhaps it was just longing magnified until it was something inhuman.

I'll admit I was startled. Perhaps petrified is a better term; I was held in place for the moment it took him to pull free of the door, rattling it on its hinges, and make a lunge for my wife.

I stepped forward and thrust at him, a good swordsman's lunge right for his guts. The blade bit something as indistinct as a heavy spider's web, but it was enough; the gray man withdrew with greater speed than his feet could have given him and snarled at me from beyond the range of my sword. Gray goo trailed from his wound to the blade of my sword, and I felt the hair on my arms and neck stand up.

Halleyne switched back to the protective song, singing, directing it at the gray intruder with the full force of her voice, repeating the sequence again and again. I could feel something crackle in the air—physical manifestation of the magical power she wielded.

The gray thing shrank back against the door, half-melding with it, and his face and chest were battered by something I could not see, as deeply and painfully as though each of Halleyne's song-notes were a stone fired from a crossbow.

Then it was gone, a little gray goo trailing after him as he escaped. Halleyne sang after him, like a victorious archer raining arrows after a fleeing foe.

And the citadel screamed.

There is no other way to express it. The fleeing gray thing wailed in despair, but his shriek was picked up all over the citadel, echoing from scores of voices. I saw dust jarred from the tops of beams overhead and felt deep vibration in the heels of my boots.

That made my stomach lurch. If whatever it was could affect the very stone beneath us . . . if the great spar extending from the mountain, on which this citadel was built, was not the reliable foundation long-dead Prince Balaquin had said it was . . . we could end up tumbling to the base of the cleft, a landslide of shaped stone and crushed nobility.

But then the shrieks faded to nothingness and
the thrumming in the earth ended, and startled
cries for answers, from human voices this time,
sounded out in the corridor.

Chapter Ten

"I assume," said General Oakwall, "that you were not too, ah, distracted to hear the commotion."

At his invitation, conveyed by a messenger, we'd joined him in his assigned quarters—a room much more spacious and better-furnished than ours—in order that the Liedan party be formed up and ready when it was time for us to conduct Elowar to the great hall.

Halleyne and I looked at each other. "Ah, yes, we heard a little of it," I said.

"Damned peculiar thing," he said. "They say the mountains are weird places."

He was not in our confidence, of course, so we did not tell him what Halleyne had told me. That in her song of searching for spirits she'd found some.

Many. More than she could count. More than she'd ever felt, except on the occasion when she'd sung to repel spirit-infected serpents by the thousands. And those serpent-spirits, she said, were tiny little things, not like the fully-developed entities she'd found with her song in Lieda and here.

No, it was as though we were in a storehouse of spirits, most of them the shrieking, pitiful trapped things she'd sensed on the trip down from Bekalli.

But some weren't trapped. Some were loose, roaming—*vengeful* was the word she'd used. Several had detected her, the little part of her that went wandering whenever she sang her song of searching. They'd come after her. She'd fled by devious musical routes back to her true mind and body . . . but one had still found her.

And it had been the spirit of a man. She thought her very recognition of the thing made it visible to us, for ghosts were supposed to be unseen.

If the preponderance of legends were to be believed, ghosts were a rare thing. Spirits of wind and wood lived on the earth, going where they wished, inhabiting the places where they had been conceived. But spirits of slain men and women were said to depart for the halls of the dead, with only the very unusual one strong or revenge-minded enough to stay behind and haunt its place of death.

She said that her pursuer was similar in the extreme to the other spirits she'd detected. If so, this new citadel was the most haunted site on the face of the world.

"Don't you think?" asked Oakwall.

"Eh?"

He smirked at us. The few times he'd spoken to us during the trip, it had usually been some comment or another on our newlywed condition. "It's high time to go, don't you think?"

Halleyne shook her head. "No, the servant said there would be a messenger to alert us that time was upon us—"

And a knock sounded on the general's door.

Elowar's chambers were on the fourth floor, on the same hall as the heavily-guarded doors marking King Jehan's suite. We were not admitted into Elowar's rooms; as soon as the general rapped on her door, she and her bodyguards emerged. We were swept up in her parade as she led the way down to the great hall. Elowar's gown, a shimmering thing in coral pink, was gorgeous—how her quartermaster had transported it intact all those days from Bekalli was beyond me—but she herself seemed pale and tight-lipped. As her bodyguards struggled to maintain pace with her, one before, one behind, the servant took us down a narrow stairwell, into the first-floor foyer, itself well-occupied by courtiers, soldiers, and representatives from four nations, and thence into the great hall.

This was indeed a huge room, occupying most of the already tall first floor of the building. It was longer to the north and south, with columns along its length and great fireplaces on each wall but the eastern. The central third of the room was two stories in height, with balconies north and south; the north balcony, directly over King Jehan's throne, was for audience, while the south balcony, overlooking the throne, was a curtained area inhabited, it was said, by watchers and archers alert for trouble.

Most of the hall was taken up by long, sturdy tables with matching benches to either side; this was to be a heavily-attended dinner. The floor was strewn with fresh straw, and in the old fashion so admired by mountain folk, there were large, shaggy dogs here and there, wagging tails and accepting caresses from the attendees already seated. They would soon enough be accepting handouts and discarded tidbits.

The throne at the head of the room was empty. So was one of the two tables nearest it; at the other was Sheroit, beside two men whose precise motions and deferential manners reminded me of court functionaries. He saw our arrival and waved us over, then dismissed the others.

He rose as we reached him. "There is no table for the Bontiniard head of state," he said. "So I have been keeping pests away from our Liedan table."

"How thoughtful of you," the queen said. Though color was still absent from her cheek, her manner had become gay once more. I knew from years of serving Lieda's royals that this was a pose; whatever had disturbed her still had her in its grip.

Once we were seated, I gestured at the empty adjacent table. "I must assume that's for the Terosai contingent."

"Yes. They will be joining us soon, I hope; I hear unfortunate rumors that Queen Thaliara is perhaps a little ill. Now—" his face became animated as he turned toward Halleyne and me— "you *must* tell me of this adventure you had, and of your survival, and whom else of that ill-fated expedition is among the living."

I started to speak but Halleyne cut me off. "We would love to, Sheroit—I'm sorry, *King* Sheroit. But we will have to do the same for King Jehan, and Queen Thaliara, and all others who have an interest in what happened to us. I think we should wait until dinner is assembled and then make one performance of it."

"Hmm. Very sensible of you. I will wait, then."
He gave me a close look. "Rumor says that you
hold me and Prince Teuper in some suspicion."

"Rumor flies even more swiftly than truth."

"How can I prove to you that it was not Teuper
and I, but the very double-spirits that assaulted
us, who did you harm?"

"I have a way you might do so. But it will have
to wait."

He made a comic face and sighed. "The song
every negotiator must sing. Wait, wait, wait. Even
as a king I wait. It's good to see the two of you
still impudent enough to feel you can tell a king
to—oh, there they are."

We turned to follow his gaze. Entering from
the main doors of the hall was a large retinue
of nobles, all garbed in Terosai fashion, with their
flowing, cumbersome garments. At the head of
the troupe stood a beautiful young woman in
yellow-gold, a modest coronet on her head, a
necklace and belt of onyx setting off the hues of
her gown. She was arm-in-arm with a tall, dark-
haired man, rugged of feature and quick of eye,
dressed in a crisp Terosai general's uniform. They
and their hangers-on came abreast of our table;
the two of them made a pleasant nod in the
general direction of Elowar and Sheroit, then all
sat at the Terosai table.

"It's Thaliara, all right," Halleyne whispered to
me. "Her portrait is all over the royal palace in
Greffon. I can't truly make out her features for
all the makeup she's wearing, but I'd swear she
was sixteen."

"How so?"

"By her build."

"That's not much of a clue," I said. "For all she's thirty, she probably—" Then whatever parts of my mind are made for discretion shut me up. I had been about to say, "she probably has had no children to spoil her figure," but it did occur to me that my dear wife, swelling with child, would probably not appreciate such a comment. So I coughed to cover for the break in my speech and continued, "probably keeps fit."

I continued, "Oh, and that's certainly Buyan with her. I saw him once when his unit was on parade, long before I went to work in the palace. Hard to tell about him, though. With features like his, a little dye in his beard, he could look much the same for twenty years. You notice they didn't come charging over to talk to us."

"Meaning either they haven't heard the rumor of Jerno's survival or they're uncommonly patient about obtaining answers."

"Lords and Ladies!"

We turned back toward the source of that call.

Standing by the throne, one to either side of it, were Teuper dar Hiaro and an older man. Each leaned against the throne, elbow up atop the back of the thing, in an identical pose, a rogue's attitude of amusement; they had obviously practiced this. They wore well-dyed garments of fine wool, clothes of mountain-clan nobles. The older man wore a crown of gold shot through with rubies that glimmered in the light from the many candles on the chandelier overhead, and his beard and hair were a solid gray; but his size and features were so much like Teuper's that there was no mistaking him. He was King Jehan, master of Hiaraniard.

The king broke his pose to stride forward. "Happy I am to welcome the most illustrious diplomatic party from Lieda. Now all are assembled for the event that has drawn us here, the wedding of Queen Thaliara of Terosalle and Buyan of Lieda—a union of two peoples, the very signature on the treaties of peace we have forged in the last half-year." He spoke with a distinct foreign accent and diction that suggested that Terosai, the language in which he addressed the gathering, was still a partial mystery to him.

"I have chosen," he continued, "not to delay proceedings with a march of precedence or any of the other trappings of more civilized courts." That got him a laugh. "We will eat; we will mingle amongst one another; we will drink. And tomorrow there will be a most wondrous wedding." He clapped his hands sharply, loud enough to be heard all over the hall, then spoke briefly with his son and seated himself on the throne. Servants ran up to him with a small table the height of his throne's arms and set it beside him. More servants entered the hall through its main doors, bearing platters of food; the scent of well-roasted meats filled the air.

"How did they get to the throne unobserved?" I whispered. "Some unseen door in that quarter of the room?"

"Nothing so mysterious," Halleyne said. "While the Terosai party was making its stately way to their table, I saw two men wrapped up full in dark cloaks trotting along the wall toward the front of the room. My purse against yours that it was Jehan and Teuper, taking advantage of a distraction the way you always do."

"No bet."

A servant appeared at our table and set before each of us a large round flatbread. The next servant used a fork to spear large slices of mutton and convey them atop the flatbread, then left the platter of mutton behind for more eventual consumption. More servants came, bearing goblets and wine and spiced steamed grains and aromatic goat-cheeses and many more things than I could keep track of. I noticed that Elowar took very little food.

And all the while, I became very aware of attention turned in our direction—specifically in Halleyne's and mine, rather than just in the direction of our table. In swelling conversation from many directions I heard our names.

I'd gotten just one slice of mutton in me when the king rose from his own plate and clapped his hands for attention. "You know it is my habit to entertain with minstrels and jugglers and freaks of nature during our dining hours. But there have been too many rumors and whispers this day— none of you would be satisfied with such disports. Therefore let me call on those who have the answers to settle all rumors, Kin Underbridge of Lieda and Lady Halleyne dar Dero of Terosalle, to tell us of their return from the deadly treaty expedition of last year. To tell us of those we have loved who might also have survived."

Everyone in the hall looked at us and fell silent. We looked at each other.

"You're the Judge," she whispered.

"You're the Bard-in-training," I said.

"I'm not even a recognized apprentice."

"Bards entertain, Judges consider."

She made an exasperated noise and stood, her smile falsely suggesting that I'd just paid her a grand compliment. "It would be my great honor," she began, "to address such an august gathering of nobles and heroes."

And she launched into the tail of our shipwreck. How we'd lain at anchor off Hanuman Point until we had forged a peace between our nations. How wind-spirits sent by some malevolent enemy, and probably intending our destruction, had swept us off the map to the islands we called Landfall. How the Terosai admiral surviving with us, Lesto dar Ostaferion, had perished at the bite of a viper . . . the very type of serpent that was to cause us so much grief later.

An idea occurred to me and I whispered, "Trade places." Relieved, she sat and began to eat as I stood and picked up her narrative. It was time, I decided, to begin setting our enemies up for the fall they must inevitably take.

I acknowledged that the Teuper and Sheroit who were stranded with us were, so far as anyone had been able to determine, double-spirits. That these spirits had taken their place while the real nobles were stranded on an island much nearer to the continent. Then I told the audience of the perfidy of the two who had been among us.

I spoke of how, as winter gripped us on the island and we struggled to build shelters and stockpile food, the Sheroit with us subtly widened the gulf between the common-born and the nobles so there would come a time of conflict between the classes. I spoke of madness claiming King Jerno, leading to him setting aside his queen and claiming a new, unwilling queen, Shallia, and suggested that the Sheroit with us could have helped me force some sense into the king's befuddled mind but did not. I spoke of the evil of Teuper, who desired Lady Halleyne, and then beat her nearly to death when she denied him, on the very day the outraged commoners broke out in revolt against the king's madness and noblemen's greed.

And it was there, I think, that I began truly to move the crowd against the Sheroit and Teuper who had been with us. I'd known mountain clansmen in the past; there were always some in the court at Bekalli, representatives of their clans. As I continued, I adopted more of their simplicity of speech and turn of phrase . . . and played to their obsessive interest in the honor of heroes.

Teuper's attack on Halleyne was the first great dishonor, and some of the mountain men pounded their tables at the appropriate points of my narrative. The second dishonor, which I spoke of with feeling, was Teuper and Sheroit letting me think Halleyne had died, when in fact she'd been carried off, injured, a heroine to the unrepentant rebels I'd been forced to exile. I never mentioned Jenina Morlin as instigator of the rebellion; it would not do to have important Liedans like General Oakwall remember her name as that of a traitor against the king.

The third dishonor I described was when, late in winter, Sheroit and Teuper summoned me out for a talk, confessed to their part in the conspiracy—with young Teuper naming Jehan as his father, and Thaliara and Buyan as willing confederates—and then tried to hold my attention while a third confederate crept out from the shadows.

Three great dishonors. In the mountain clan scheme of justice, I'd just tried and convicted these double-spirits who had taken Teuper's and Sheroit's place. To the clans, a dishonored warrior was something to be chased away or slaughtered. I breezed through the fight that resulted from the ambush, dismissing the way I'd killed their confederate as a minor consideration, but making sure to mention the injury I'd done to Teuper, a knife-blow that had pierced his left side, perhaps his left lung. I suggested it was only the double-Teuper's spirit powers that allowed him to survive as he and the double-Sheroit fled the island.

I caught sight of Halleyne. She was nodding, approving; she knew what I was about. Then she said, "Trade places," and I thankfully sat.

"You've grown uncommonly well-spoken," whispered Sheroit.

"I have been in the company of fine speakers and those who steer the course of opinion," I said, nodding to indicate he was among them.

Halleyne told of their exile on Turtlehead Island. How one of their number, Daneeth Po, became mad and allied himself with the Snake-Mother, serpent goddess of the island. How he desired to have everyone bitten by the Gloriana vipers, whose venom made their victims thralls of Snake-Mother. I found it interesting that she did not mention the little spirits in the venom, the actual effectors of that thralldom.

She spoke of my efforts to reach the island, making of them a hero's journey, until I had to keep myself from squirming in embarrassment. Sheroit, I could see, was amused by my discomfiture. She spoke of Daneeth Po leading hordes of writhing serpents in assault after assault on the Turtlehead encampment while they waited for my return with new-built rafts to carry them to safety. She told of the assault we made on Snake-Mother's buried temples, and of Shallia dar Kantrin's mastery of Bardic magic techniques that allowed her to soothe Snake-Mother back into a troubled sleep. I saw a Terosai Bard in the audience perk up at the thought that one of their own might have achieved that level of power in the absence of Bardic officials. And I noted that, again, Halleyne spoke not at all of the spirits in the venom, nor of how the Bardic songs and magic they'd used were designed to repel spirits.

I stood to take the final refrain of our story. King Jerno's return to sanity during these troubled times. The dual wedding a day before our departure. But our return I attributed to the masterful sailing skills of Jenina Morlin, not to a wind-spirit summoned by Halleyne. So long as she wanted to keep her spirit-magic a secret, I would help conceal it. In my tale, I skipped over the events from our arrival at Hanuman Point to our reaching Bekalli, leaving the audience with the impression that we rowed an outrigger canoe into Bekalli Harbor.

I sat at last, and we received the table-banging applause of the audience. Between us, we'd managed to tell the tale and eat most of a dinner in the meantime.

An immediate hubbub of noise and conversation swelled as the applause died, but Thaliara's voice cut through it. "So the last you knew, my mother was alive and well?" Her expression was one of longing and hope—masterfully played, I thought.

"She was," Halleyne said, and stood. She moved to stand beside Thaliara and drew from her pouch a much-folded piece of paper. "She bade me give this to you."

With fingers trembling, Queen Thaliara unfolded the paper and read what was written upon it. Finally, her voice breaking, she said, "Listen to these words. It is dated less than three moons ago, and is in my mother's hand. 'Dearest daughter, it is with a great sense of accomplishment that I inform you that I yet live.' Skipping a bit, she tells of much that you've just heard from the lips of Halleyne—aha! *Thalahai* Halleyne, congratulations on your title, and I do confirm it—and Kin. Then, 'My representative and her retinue will have, by now, dispatched a ship to bring the rest of us off this prison—' True?"

Halleyne nodded.

"'And soon we will be reunited.' More personal words for me, and then she has set her seal to it." I could see tears run down Thaliara's face, spoiling her makeup. "Halleyne, thank you for the joy you have brought me." She turned back to the room. "My mother lives!"

There was another outburst of applause. Mine was among the loudest, though none knew it was for the hand Halleyne had just played. Thaliara still had not figured it out. Nor had Buyan; I expected him to lean over and point out what she'd missed, but the royal bastard just sat there beaming for his bride-to-be.

Halleyne curtsied and turned away to rejoin me. She was between the tables when I saw the thought penetrate Thaliara's mind like too-late lightning. "Halleyne," she called.

My wife turned.

Thaliara's voice wavered just a bit. "I was still thought dead when my mother wrote this. How did she come to address a letter to me?"

Halleyne smiled. "I do not know, Majesty." She curtsied again and rejoined me, still smiling, her satisfaction genuine.

I whispered to her, "She's just figuring out that you rammed her and hulled her."

For the suspicion had to have been planted in the minds of many people present that Queen Lia addressed a letter to her daughter because she, Lia, believed Thaliara to have been one of the conspirators, believed that Thaliara would naturally have emerged to claim the throne after Lia had been disposed of. These people need not know that Halleyne's pouch contained similar letters to other nobles Queen Lia thought might have seized control of Terosalle once she was gone.

I felt very successful. I'd fostered contempt for the "false" Sheroit and Teuper. I had to prove that it had been the real Sheroit and Teuper with us to unleash that contempt, though. Halleyne had fostered suspicion of Thaliara's complicity in this conspiracy; again, we had to prove our facts before we could do real damage to Thaliara's reign. But it was a good start.

King Jehan, from his throne, called out, "*Thal-ahai* Halleyne, Judge Kin, your story changes the lines of the map of our rule with almost every word you speak. What of King Jerno? What is he to be now that he has returned?"

Elowar stood. "It is actually for me to explain that, Majesty. I have come to terms with my former husband. He confirms the treaties and proclamations I have made, such as our alliance of nations, and I confirm his, such as his elevation of Kin here to the status of Judge of Lieda. However, the union between me and Jerno is done."

Sheroit betrayed little, but I saw him sag just a bit, in relief I thought.

"We cannot rule together, of course. We might for a time, king and queen of old—but should one of us wed there would be three rulers, should both wed, four—and then a war to determine whose would be the line of succession. We need no more wars. So one of us has chosen to step down as ruler of Lieda. It was I."

Sheroit's face froze, shock and even outrage manifest on it. And I swore to myself, for Elowar, speaking to King Jehan, could not see the man betray himself. All I'd set up with her was undone. She'd done it wrong, and I silently cursed her foolishness.

Then I saw Burslan, Jehan and Elowar's pet mage, royal advisor on matters magical, sensor of mystic interferences, chaser-away of ticks and bedbugs. So long as I'd known him he had never confessed to his family name and had spoken perhaps a hundred words to me.

His full attention was on Sheroit's face, recording every expression and twitch. Elowar had set her second pair of eyes on Sheroit's face that she might be free to perform her task. I almost sighed aloud in relief.

And finally I emerged from these thoughts enough to hear the roar of conversation erupting in the hall, a hundred voices speaking at a time in a handful of languages, as the assembled nobles tried to make sense of what Elowar had just said.

She was still speaking: " . . . now a formal principality of Lieda, and I am its princess. As of some days ago, Jerno rules again from Bekalli . . . but all we have striven to do in forging treaties and alliances is still intact." She managed a rather wicked smile. "And since my former husband desires new children, I can only think that there will soon be caravans of eager, wide-hipped young noblewomen hurrying to Bekalli, longing for formal introductions." She sat.

Sheroit, his expression recovered, leaned across the table to grip her hands in his. "I congratulate you," he said. "You are free of vengeful thoughts, and now free of ruling and re-making a nation that has long been shaped in the form of Jerno. I think you've made a deal that well suits you." He oozed sincerity.

"I am pleased you approve," she said. "It was not something I could consult with you about beforehand. It will lead to . . . no changes?"

"None."

She smiled at him and then glanced at Burslan. The mage's expression gave nothing away. She glanced at his hand atop the table; I saw he had three fingers balled as if in a fist, but his forefinger and middle finger were stretched out on the table. A signal.

I saw Elowar swallow. She squeezed Sheroit's hands before releasing them. "Ah! Kin, be a dear, fetch the tray of fruits for me."

"Proof!" That was a roar, in the mountain dialect of Terosai, from the back of the hall. I saw a big, middle-aged war-chief standing. He was nearly as

hairy as a mountain bear, and had not much
dressed up for the event; he wore leathers well-
suited to horseback riding, though they were
pulled open against the heat of the hall, but there
was enough gold on his fingers and around his
neck to attest to his noble status. His black beard
bristled as he spoke. "Underbridge brought proof
of his story when he took King Jerno to Bekalli.
I've nosed about. It's true. Many have seen Jerno
alive. Queen Elowar has seen him. What proof
does the young heir offer that he wasn't the
conspirator, the wind-summoner?"

Eyes turned to young Teuper, who sat among
the Terosai. He stood and smiled. "Chief—I'm
sorry, *Baron* Loneyt is still aggrieved on behalf
of the Red Lances—"

"The Red Lances should have been mine! Your
father cannot hand them over to that girl—"

"Yes, he can." Teuper's voice was quite reasonable. "We live in a new time. Things are being
done differently. And look at the result: old
enemies dining together, mostly amicably." That
drew some laughs, though not from the black-
bearded chief. "Your Rockfall Clan is a mighty
and noble clan, Loneyt. It would not be improved
by the addition of the Red Lances survivors.
You've lost nothing."

"I want proof."

Teuper sighed and appealed to me and Halleyne.
"You, too. There is still suspicion in your voices.
Do you want proof?"

That irritated me. I knew we'd done a fine job
of concealing our suspicion of Teuper, putting all
blame on his supposed spirit-double. Teuper was
anticipating our true thoughts. Then I felt better;

he was doing so because he knew he was guilty of the crimes we described.

Halleyne said, "We've not demanded any. But we would certainly not refuse it. What proof do you offer?"

"What do you want?"

I leaned over to the mage Burslan. "You can tell when magic has altered flesh—changed its markings, removed scars?"

He nodded.

"I stabbed the Teuper I knew," I said, loud enough for all in the hall to hear. "A good blow, made worse by his incompetence as a fighter." Did I see his face tighten just a bit? "A double-spirit might not carry a scar, but a man would. If you carry no scar where I stabbed my Teuper, then you are obviously not the one I knew. Bare your flesh, and I will look; Burslan here can see through deceptions my eyes cannot detect."

Teuper wavered a bit. "But I do have scars. I've not exactly led a pampered life—"

Some laughed at that, including his own father on the throne.

"Well," he continued, "perhaps I'm not scarred where you would damn me for it." He rose and came to our table; then, with an energetic bound, he leaped up on the end of it and began undoing the buttons on his tunic. "As I bare all," he said, "I will remind the noble fathers of beautiful daughters that I am still unwed . . ."

More laughter. He shucked off his tunic and handed it to General Oakwall. This left him bare from the waist up, and he raised his arms for the assembly, that all might have a better look at him. He was well-formed and received some applause.

Thaliara herself looked on with interest. Then Teuper knelt on the table, between platters of mutton and gamefowl, before the royal party of Lieda.

I carefully looked at the left upper quarter of his chest. There was a scar high, near the collar-bone. But in the palm-sized area where my blade had to have pierced him moons ago, along the ribs, the flesh was tanned and unmarred.

I looked at Burslan. He said, "No magic has molded his flesh. No magic to blur the senses. He does reek of spells, but not of those types."

"Every prince should carry wards to protect him," Teuper said. "I also reek of cologne. Are you satisfied?"

I looked to Halleyne. But her eyes were closed. My ears, long keyed for the pitch of her voice, heard her humming the "Spring Hunting Song" again.

"Well?" said Teuper.

I returned my attention to him. Again I spoke loudly enough for the room to hear—it would not be good to have them think me a poor loser. "I am satisfied," I said, and tried to make it sound happy.

Applause. I was growing sick of applause.

Teuper retrieved his tunic from the general and began donning it again. "I'll tell you a secret," he said, his voice low enough that only those at the table could hear it.

"Do tell."

"I did lose a battle to you. The short time I knew Halleyne aboard ship—" Halleyne's eyes opened but she did not stop humming. "—was enough for me to love her. When Sheroit and I were stranded and I thought her lost, I was destroyed. And now I know she lives, she is still lost to me. You need not seek any vengeance of me; you have been cruel enough already." His buttoning done, he leaped down from our table to seat himself again among the Terosai.

Halleyne was pale.

"Are you well?"

"Get me out of here. I am going to be sick."

Chapter Eleven

Doubt assailed me as we returned to our room. Was the well-spoken, love-struck youth who had been on the table before me actually innocent of the crime I'd accused him of? How could he not be, when he bore no mark of my injury to him, and no sign that such a mark had been mystically erased?

And Halleyne, pale, unspeaking, leaned heavily against me as we walked, but would not tell me what ailed her. My stomach, already ill-served by the test Teuper had won, tied itself up in knots.

Our room was empty, stripped bare. I asked a servant where our packs had been taken. She led us back through the halls we'd traversed so she could ask a higher-ranking servant, then took us up a flight of stairs to a much larger room with finer furniture, rugs on the floor, a tapestry on the wall.

I settled Halleyne on the bed. She was obviously in distress, gulping constantly, holding her hands crossed over her belly. "Tell me what to do," I said, begging. "What to bring you."

The door was thrown open. Into the room strode the black-bearded chief, Loneyt. "I must speak with you."

"Get out," I said. It came out a snarl.

"I must speak with you."

I launched myself at him, my open hand catching him midchest; off-balance, he staggered backwards, into the hall, slamming into the wall opposite, me still with him. Anger blazed in his eyes and he reached for the knife at his belt; but it was no longer there. I held it so its point pricked his throat.

"Did I ask you to come in?" I asked. "No. Did I ask you to set your needs above my wife's? No. Yet you do anyway. Can I think of any reason not to ram this through your throat? No."

"Kin?" Halleyne called. "I will be all right. You can let him in."

I gave Loneyt a look suggesting that manners would be a good investment for him, then stood aside to let him pass. I did not hand him back his knife. Once we were inside, I barred the door behind us.

Halleyne did look a little better. Still pale, she was at least no longer gulping.

Loneyt said, "Hey, ah, hey," and tossed a little pinch of what looked like dust into one corner. He glanced at us as though to make sure of our interpretation of this; but I'd seen Burslan do much the same thing many times for King Jerno and knew what he was about. He repeated the procedure for the other three corners . . . and I could feel the very quality of the air change, muting sounds.

"Little things we learn to remain chieftain," he said. "Now no one can hear. These rooms, nobles' rooms, full of ears."

"What do you want?" I said.

"The Red Lances' chieftainship."

"I gathered that. But I have nothing to do with it."

"If Jehan falls, it will be mine."

"You're not one of the chiefs sworn to him?"

He shrugged. "I have sworn. So when I break with him, I will tell him first that I renounce my oath. The honorable way."

"I still don't see what we have to do with it."

"The boy. Teuper. The first moon he was back, he was always with the healers. So my cousins in the Red Lances tell me."

"Not too odd for someone who'd been stranded for moons without enough food."

"Yes. But his healers don't speak of what they were doing for him. Why? There is no shame to starvation. One of his healers died, fell off a cliff. Why?"

"Because as rocks fall, so do people?"

With an expression of distaste, he waved away my words.

Halleyne's eyes narrowed as she looked at him. "You want to know if we have learned of any weakness among Jehan's strengths."

"Yes."

"We'll consider it. But first, I want to know about the ceremony. The one that bound you to Jehan."

He shook his head. "The usual chief's oath. Greater chief, lesser chief. Only he calls us barons."

"No, before that. The secret one. The one that truly bound you to him."

"There was none."

"Why did you join him?"

"When you smell smoke in the wind, you head away from the fire."

"Meaning he would have crushed you if you hadn't joined. Are the other chiefs the same way? Those who joined him first?"

He shook his head. "They fear him."

"Yet they are strong and vital."

He just stared at her . . . and I became aware he was holding his breath. Finally, he said, "Yes. Too young. Too vital. Beyond their years. I do not know why. Only that it is recent."

"Very well. Tell us what you want, all of it."

"I am chief of the Rockfalls. My mother's brother and later his son were chiefs of the Red Lances. Cenpeydon, whom they say must have been owner of many face-scars, for he always wore a helmet, killed my cousin and became chief. The Red Lances accepted him as their new chief. That's fair." He shrugged. "Then Cenpeydon died without issue, killed by Jehan. Black Rocks slaughtered the Red Lances until only thirty were left. Jehan issued the chieftainship to the girl, Sora. She was originally Black Rock, not Red Lance. She was among them as nurse to Thaliara. I am the only one left with Red Lance chieftain's blood; the clan should be mine."

"What does it give you?"

"Old land holdings recognized by clans. Most of all, I have two sons, both good and strong and smart. They will kill one another some day to be chief of Rockfalls . . ."

"Unless," I said, "you first make one of them chief of the Red Lances."

He nodded.

"Why have you not disposed of the girl Sora?"

I asked. Halleyne shot me an offended glance, but I waved it down; such tactics were even more common among the mountain clans than among flatland nations.

"She is protected by Jehan. He is very attentive."

Halleyne asked, "Are they lovers?"

He shrugged. "Maybe. Not in public. They embrace much, though. Listen. I don't make treaties. I make friends. Alliances. You help me take the Red Lances chieftainship, you make a friend of me. You help Jehan, you make an enemy of me. In the middle, you are nothing to me."

"Fair enough," I said, then turned to Halleyne. "Anything more?"

"No."

I handed the chief back his knife and he left without another word. I barred the door behind him.

"Are you well?"

"I am now," she said. "But I truly was sick back in the great hall."

"Why?"

"Because of the spirits."

She explained. "There's a spirit, like those whose presence I've been feeling, *within Teuper.*"

"Inside him."

"Yes, like a, like a . . ." She struggled to describe it. "Tapeworm."

"That's a vile image. What's it doing?"

"Nothing. It is trapped like the others I felt. Teuper's body is its coffin. And, worse, there are three within Elowar. The very three, I think, I felt throughout our trip. I performed my song of searching while they were right there—Burslan saying that Teuper was full of magic suggested it to me—and I could feel them, in him and in Elowar. And many others nearby."

"Presumably within the bodies of others present."

"Yes. That's what made me ill. The thought of it. Their presence. Their screaming."

I stood away from her a moment to consider. "All right. I have an idea. Tell me when I go astray.

"Jehan is creating youth for his minions, not by magic that changes the flesh, not by appealing to the gods, but by tearing youth itself from one person and putting it in another. Youth that comes with its former owner's very spirit."

"I'm not a trained mage, Kin. But with the Gloriana serpents, we saw how spirits can be moved from one being to another. Carrying traits with them."

"So spirits bearing youth are moved from one person to another. What happens to the person to whom the spirit originally belonged?"

"He would . . ." She looked down. "I suppose he would be dead."

"What about the notes, the spell you use to repulse spirits? What would happen if you were right there to direct it against one of these trapped things?"

"I don't know. Either it would eventually flee, or it is bound so tight that it cannot."

"We need to find out where this is happening."

"Where what is happening? The spirit transfer?"

"Yes. You've detected so many spirits here, loose and trapped, that I feel the transfer must take place here. Hairy Loneyt there didn't know anything about it, and he has cousins—that is to say, spies—here in the citadel. So it has to be happening out of sight."

She gave me a smirk. "You could rap the walls and search for secret ways."

"Don't be so superior. King Jehan has to have at least a bolt-hole, in case the citadel is taken— as sneaky as he is, there's little doubt of it. Obviously he needs more than that; he needs a place where he can effect this spirit-transfer ritual."

"What about the caves you spoke of? The ones Prince Balaquin used for storage."

I thought about it. "It could be. If I estimate rightly, the wall of the mansion would have been built against the entryways, covering them over."

I threw open the window shutters. Night had fallen and a light snowfall had begun, but even here some light came from the bracketed watch-torches on the wall towers.

Straight ahead I faced the slope of the western mountain. Though we'd been given much better quarters, all the best guest rooms, the ones with the most beautiful mountain views, were doubtless already filled. Ours were still at the back of the mansion, facing the mountainside itself.

I looked down, trying to cast back in my memory for images of the mountain slope as it used to be. Halleyne joined me. I pointed: "The cave entrance would have been there, toward the center of the mansion wall, at ground level."

"Near where the central chimney is."

"Yes."

"Could there be a way through the fireplace there?"

"In the great hall?" I thought about it, then shook my head. "Impractical, especially if he wanted to keep it a secret. He couldn't enter it at all if the fire were going—"

"Perhaps the fireplace slides out or aside."

"Dear, I don't think you could budge a fireplace that size with anything short of a mule team. Also, he couldn't enter it any time there were people in the great hall, which would be most of the time. And as far as I can recall, the fireplaces were the only architectural features on that wall that lent themselves to disguising doors or hatches."

"Oh." She leaned out further to peer. "Well, what about the chimney?"

"What, climb down the chimney? A good way to catch a case of blacksmith's lung and ruin all your clothes."

"There's nothing to say that the chimney doesn't have two compartments. One full of smoke, one not. See how broad it is?"

"Yes, and the other two chimneys as well. Wouldn't a chimney concealing a bolt-hole be broader than one not?"

"Not if they were designed to look alike in dimension and form. One with a bolt-hole, two with wasted space. Or maybe bolt-holes of their own."

"Good point." I leaned out to stare up the wall of the mansion. Wooden, few projections, windows every so often. The stone chimney itself would be an easier climb—were I still a light-boned boy who could climb like a monkey.

"You're not thinking what I fear you are," she said.

"No. Even if I could scale that, I fear I'd find nothing but chimney at the top. I need to find a proper entrance to his bolt-hole, and his quarters are bound to be guarded still. But it does occur to me—if I remember right, Jehan's quarters are on this side of the fourth floor . . . a curious choice for a man who could have chosen the suite with the best view over his citadel. For some reason, he chose for his quarters to be against that chimney."

"What about the floor below? Our floor. There might be an entrance here."

"I'll find out." I closed the shutters.

"And I with you."

"You're sure you won't become ill again?"

"No."

I measured, by pacing, the nearest approach to that central chimney. This put me within a couple of paces of a door much like the one to our own quarters. I looked up and down the hall to make sure no one was approaching, then gave a quiet knock.

There was no response. I pulled up on the lever that would raise the bar on the other side, but it slid without engaging the mechanism.

Therefore someone was inside, perhaps sleeping.

I cursed. This was a good, well-engineered door. It was set within a frame that fit it well, and on the inside was a second, narrower frame that meant it could only open outward . . . and meant also that no knife blade, no matter how narrow, could be slid in to raise the bar. "Do you have string?" I asked.

"In our room."

"Would you fetch some? Eight or ten paces' worth at least."

No one came through the hallway while she was gone. I thanked the gods that the great feast was still going on downstairs. When she returned with the string, I slid one end up over the top of the door and crammed more in as fast as I could until Halleyne, stooping and peering underneath the door, announced that it had reached the ground on the far side. With her knife, she dragged it back through. I tied a loop in that end and fitted the other end through it, drawing it nearly closed. Thus we had a lasso of string wrapped around the door top to bottom.

"I doubt we will pull the door down with that," she said.

"You've lost faith in me." I drew the string at the top of the door to the left, until it was past the top-left corner of the door and in the left gap between door and frame. I directed her to do the same with the string at the bottom. Then all we had to do was draw the string taut . . . and we had a lasso around the bar itself. Quietly, carefully, I pulled up on the fragile cord and felt the bar slide upward. A moment later its movement was stopped and I could pull the door open.

Darkness beyond. Halleyne fetched a candle from one of the wall brackets in the hall and we entered.

It was half bedroom, half library; it had a bed, a fireplace, a stand-up closet against the wall; the rest of the walls were concealed by bookshelves. There were more books here than any place I'd seen other than the Bekalli palace library. There was no one in the bed. I retrieved the string and shut the door, then lowered the bar back in place.

"Well, we know there is a bolt-hole from this room," Halleyne said.

I nodded. Unless the person who owned the room used the same sort of string-trick we had in order to enter, he or she had left by means not yet visible.

We went to work searching. I examined the fireplace—which was cold, though its ashes hadn't been swept out—while Halleyne searched the bookcase to one side and the closet to the other. We handed the candle back and forth as we needed it.

In the closet, Halleyne said, "It's a woman. A small one with a taste for bright colors. What do you want to bet it's Sora?"

"I no longer want to bet with you. You intimidate me."

"Coward. I—oh, I've found something."

There was a faint little thump from within the closet. I looked over; she was sitting inside the thing, for only her legs protruded. And now the closet rose a full pace up in the air, majestically, as if carried up by unseen ghosts . . . and then stopped.

I stepped around in front. She peered at me, a bit wide-eyed, from between hanging gowns and dresses. "Did I find it?" she asked.

"I believe so." I knelt down to look underneath the closet, waving the candle, and illuminated a hole in the wall, less than a pace square, almost at ground level. "You did."

"Help me down."

I did, then crawled under the closet, enjoining her not to play with switches until I was clear. The hole led to a stone shaft, running up and down, with iron staples as thick as my thumb hammered into the stone on one side to form rungs of a ladder. The candle revealed a lever beside the first rung down. "With logic and mathematics," I said, "we have found the bolt-hole."

"Finding it isn't enough."

"Then I'll go first."

I chose to descend; up would be Jehan's quarters, so down would be chambers he chose to conceal. Halleyne crawled in carefully behind me, and once she was within the shaft she examined the lever, then pulled it down. I heard the closet make a quiet rumble of descent and then thump against the floor.

Down I climbed, and counted twenty rungs spaced half a pace apart. About halfway down, the stones behind my back began to grow warm, and the heat was oppressive by the time I reached the bottom of the shaft. There was a wall of bricks to my left—directly against the face of the mountain, unless my sense of direction had gone completely awry—and a doorway-sized hole allowing some fresher air to emerge and cool me. Halleyne joined me and we pushed on.

Directly into the cave entrance I remembered. That was a jolt of memory; I half-expected to see Prince Balaquin, merry with his planning for a grand citadel, jotting notes on a slateboard and asking what I thought of some design that was beyond my skills to critique. But no, this outer cave was now filled with scores of large burlap bags piled against the walls.

"What's that odor?" She wrinkled her nose against it. "Musty."

"From the bags, I think. Let's not look until we know what else we're facing." I led the way through the back reaches of the cave, to the opening to what we'd called the Gallery, a longer, straighter cave chamber. It was here we'd planned to quarter ourselves if the weather went bad, all those years ago.

Now, the light from Halleyne's candle picked out strange shapes and furnishings. Cages of metal against the back wall, four of them abreast. Shelves upon which lay weapons and riding packs. And in the center of the chamber, something I had never seen before. We approached it.

It had started out as a large table or slab—a torturer's table, for there were chains and manacles at both ends. There was now a body in the chains, a man, shriveled like the mountain-clans' dead when they are mummified by cold arid air. He wore the garments of a mountain clansman. On his mummy's face was an anguished expression that indicated that he was awake and aware when he died.

The whole tabletop lay beneath a curved lid made of glass and wood. Into a wooden framework were laid small panes of glass, each a quarter-pace square, so that this lid was like some curved, coffin-sized window. I saw that hinges held it to one side of the table.

An array of glass tubes penetrated the underside of the table near the victim's feet. The tubes curled downward and ended in a second box, wood on bottom but all glass elsewhere, nearly a pace square, resting on the floor. That box had hinges on one facing so that it might be opened, but there was nothing in it.

With all the glass, the cost of making—and repairing—such a thing must have been fantastic. The whole thing stank of the musty smell we'd detected in the outer cave, and it was very sharp here.

Halleyne said, "It looks like . . . like . . ."

"A still," I told her. The words were out of my mouth before I could contain them: "They're distilling spirits."

Halleyne glared at me. Then she closed her eyes and hummed the notes of the spirit-seeking song. Her eyes snapped open. "There are spirits here. Wandering. Half a dozen within a stone's throw. I have to be careful or I will draw them to me."

"I wonder why they are wandering."

"Rejected perhaps? Perhaps they escaped the binding-magic?"

Something about the corpse on the table drew my attention. "Look here."

She peered where I was pointing: at the body's bare chest, along its left side. It looked as though the victim had sustained a grievous wound; that side of its chest was caved in as though by a mighty blow.

We both heard a distant grating sound, then a low metallic clang: the very noise I had made several times when descending the iron ladder.

No good place to hide here in the Gallery. We scurried to the outer chamber. I found a place where the bags on the floor were laid out in rows and we hid ourselves between two stacks of them. Halleyne snuffed the candle. The musty scent did emanate from the bags.

A glow appeared in the opening in the brick wall and grew brighter. The ringing of rungs drew closer. Moments later, King Jehan, a lamp swinging in his hand, emerged from the entryway. I was surprised to see the light from the lamp illuminate another entryway, to his left and low to the ground as he entered; this second hole had to go beneath the fireplace.

Jehan looked aggrieved. He turned to wait, and then emerged Sora, her expression composed. She headed straight for the Gallery. Then came Prince Teuper, who looked a bit abashed. They all sweated a bit from their recent proximity to the heated back of the chimney.

"Do, undo, do, undo," complained the king.

Teuper shrugged. "I can't help it. It's tickling. Growing restless. It's worse ever since we all got sick. It's not supposed to move, is it?"

Sora called back, "It's not Teuper's fault, Father. It was done in haste. We'll pull it out and give him a proper one later."

"We don't need a proper one," Teuper said, following the girl. "We've had the test, Under-bridge lost, it's done. Just pull it."

The king brought up the rear, still unhappy. "Don't be an idiot. He might contrive for another look in a less public forum. Then where would you be? Sora, child, can you bind this one in tighter so it doesn't worry Teuper?"

She was within the Gallery now, and called back, "I think so. If not, we've many new guests to choose from if we have to give him a new one. I still worry about the blow they all felt. Here, help me move these remains so we can put Teuper on the table."

They were all in the Gallery for long moments. I heard lifting and shoving. Then Teuper emerged with a burlap bag over his shoulder. He handled it with fair ease; it must have weighed about the same as a sack of seed of middle size.

He came near us, then gave the bag a heave and tossed it in our direction. It hit the stack of sacks immediately before us and they all tumbled onto us.

No great weight to them, but we held our breath, fearful of being exposed. We didn't need to worry; Teuper turned and reentered the Gallery.

One of the bags slid further down and its contents partially emerged from the top. It was another body, half-mummified, reeking of the mustiness of this cave, and it lay directly atop me, staring at me almost accusingly. I felt Halleyne shudder. I'm sure I did the same.

Chapter Twelve

We could only faintly hear their conversation inside the Gallery, snatches of sentences: "Lie down . . . lot of trouble, boy . . . damned Elowar . . . think Jerno can be turned? He could stand for a spot of youth . . . hold still."

Then chanting in Sora's voice, a tongue unknown to me. The chanting rose to a climax and ended. A minute or two later, the three of them emerged and headed for the way out. Teuper was cheerful but, interestingly, a thin trail of gray smoke rose from his hair and from the collar of his tunic. "All better," he said. "No itching at all."

"Father," said Sora, "what's to be done with this announcement of Elowar's?"

The king shrugged. "She has nothing more to offer us. Jerno's in the saddle of Lieda. We'll tell Sheroit to choose—" His further words were lost to me as they began climbing out of sight.

When they were well gone, a full minute after the distant grating noise announced that they'd closed their doorway, I threw the revolting mass of bagged bodies off me and stood, hauling Halleyne to her feet. In the blackness, I could hear her gulping for fresher air. I held her close to me and eventually felt her relax.

Finally, she said, "I kept the candle."

"A moment, then." I released her and fumbled at my belt-pouch. I came up with flint from the pouch and my belt-knife and struck them together; sparks briefly illuminated where she held the candle, and a moment later we once again had light. We wasted little time getting out of the midst of the bagged bodies.

"Can you manage a bit more exploration?" I asked.

She nodded. "I felt Sora binding that spirit. She was affixing it into Teuper's body, I think. Her strength is no greater than my own . . . I wonder if I could tear free what she has tied. And do you know why she was doing the binding?"

We moved to the eastern exit from this chamber. I directed her to hold the candle to the second passage we'd briefly seen a few minutes before. This was another hole with iron rungs, but cut from living stone rather than made of stone blocks; it descended into darkness. "The damage to the body that the spirit came from. Their method can transfer not only youth with spirits, but appearance as well."

"Yes. They made sure the unwounded appearance of that man's chest lay atop Teuper's injury. Not an illusion, a . . ."

"Patch."

I began climbing down. These rungs went down three paces, no more; then a horizontal shaft, a mere pace and a half in diameter, headed eastward and a little downward through solid stone. Rough planks were laid on the floor, and the rough appearance of the shaft said that little effort had been made to make it an easy passage for a traveler.

Halleyne joined me. I took the candle and began crawling along those planks. "I think we need to tell Elowar to make herself valuable to them again."

"By disclosing the terms of her divorce from Jerno."

"Yes."

This passage was not a long one—twenty, twenty-five paces at most. It ended in a slightly larger hollowed chamber, not quite tall enough to stand in. Iron rungs were driven into the walls here, too, but not for climbing; on the floor were coils of knotted ropes, one end of each tied off to a metal rung.

And in the center of the floor was a wooden hatch of the sort common to naval vessels. It was dogged shut.

I returned the candle to Halleyne, then held one of the metal rungs, undogged the hatch, and pulled it open. Chill wind gushed in and blew out the candle's flame. It came as no surprise to me that I stared out over emptiness, thirty or forty paces straight down. Beneath me was the moonlit snowy-stony ground of the pass. I could, if I wished, spit straight down at a cluster of Terosai tents. "The bolt-hole," I said. "Wish we could use it now."

I spent several revolting minutes going through bag after bag of bodies. I took a few things and reflected that I might be the first judge of Lieda who was also a grave-robber.

Then we ascended the rung ladder back toward

Sora's room, but this presented us with a quandary. What if she were there?

"It's not likely," Halleyne said. "The feast must still be ongoing. She will have returned to it . . . probably."

I climbed past and found what had to be the entrance to King Jehan's room. It looked much the same, a small hole for egress and a lever to pull to move whatever blocked it. Though Sora's room was not guarded, it occurred to me that Jehan's might be, even when the room was otherwise unoccupied. The rungs continued up further, though, and I went where they did.

They ended against the roof of the mansion; I could hear wind on the other side of the sloped wood above me. This, too, was a hatch, with another staple of iron and a knotted rope handy for the king's escape. But there was no other entry into the mansion.

I returned to Halleyne. "You take the candle, I'll take the knife, and if Sora's in there, we'll just have to subdue her."

She nodded and threw the lever.

I was into Sora's room as fast as scrambling hands and knees would carry me. But it was dark. I groped my way to her bed; it was still cold. When Halleyne followed with the candle, it was obvious that Sora was nowhere about.

Many minutes later, sponged off to remove the worst of the rank mummy smell, in new clothes to replace the ones we'd ruined with all that crawling, we returned to the feast. It was going nearly as strong as before, with many of the feasters just starting their third and fourth courses.

Jehan was back on his throne; Sheroit dar Bontine stood beside him and they talked intently. Teuper and Sora were at their respective seats.

We sat beside Elowar again. "Do you feel better?" she asked Halleyne.

"No. . . . I fear for you, Majesty."

"It's Highness, now that my abdication has been announced. Why fear for me?"

Halleyne's face showed the regret she felt at making this sad revelation. "King Jehan is now telling Sheroit to abandon his courtship of you. Sheroit will talk to you sometime soon to tell you that his heart has strayed, or demands of his new office call for him to marry another, or some such rot."

"You lie." Elowar's face lost all emotion. She should have been furious.

"As soon as this happens," I said, "you should have one of your retinue, in ordinary conversation with someone of the king's retinue, mention that you have the right to choose Jerno's successor. Then, later that day, one of two things will happen. Either Sheroit will come to you in a mad storm of passion, saying that he repents of his earlier foolishness and loves you more than even the sound of his own voice, or King Jehan will attempt to impose his will on you directly; probably by threatening to strip away the youth he has given you."

"Kin Underbridge, you are the most loathsome, manipulative wretch ever to serve the crown."

"Majesty—Highness—Sheroit and I are alike in important ways. We both get most of our results by manipulating the actions of others. We are both fond of you. Neither of us is in love with you." I took a deep breath. "But unlike him and those who conspire with him, I do not place too many things above life itself. They will kill the innocent for kingship and for many lesser things. The very youthfulness you carry is at the cost of lives. Three people died to restore you to youth, to fertility. Halleyne and I have seen the tools Jehan's conspiracy used to effect this."

The queen turned to Halleyne, who nodded soberly.

"Please tell me what they did to make you young," I asked. "What you saw. What you felt."

She considered. "He sent Sora to me as his ambassador of peace. Youth was a reward for coming to terms. I had her demonstrate first on another woman past childbearing years—my son Jernin's wet nurse. She was restored and happily with child within weeks. So I agreed."

"What is Sheroit to Jehan? They have some tie they have not revealed to me."

"Sheroit is originally of the Black Rock Clan." Elowar shrugged. "He confessed it to me in the early days of our courtship. His father Byrark is a long-sighted man who arranged to have him educated in Lieda and Terosalle. Jehan did much the same with his own child, sending Teuper to Terosalle."

"How was it done?" Halleyne asked. "The youthening."

"A drink, nothing more. A tankard full of clear liquid, like water, but almost silvery in the way it reflected light. And always in motion, dancing. It was tasteless yet somehow rich all at once . . . and after a day of violent illness, I was as you see me today." She shook her head to clear away the memory and looked at me, emotionless. "Kin, you have offered me too much pain to be anything but a loyal ally or a most hateful enemy." She rose.

The rest of us rose with her. Her head a bit lowered, she swept away without another word, her retinue around her like a protective shield. I saw the motion had caught King Jehan's eye, and Sheroit's; they did not cease their conversation, but followed Elowar with their gaze as she left.

Halleyne said, "I wish we could offer her something but knowledge of the way those she loves have betrayed her."

"If anything occurs to you, tell me."

As we lay together sleepless, Halleyne whispered, "Have you a plan? I don't."

"No. Well, first, Elowar might have me killed for causing her so much misery, in which case I won't need one."

"Don't say such things even in jest. Besides, even if she wanted you dead, you'd just talk her out of it. You *are* like Sheroit in many ways."

"Don't say such things even in jest. Listen, sweet, all I've truly wanted to do here is open Elowar's eyes, which is now happening, and to find out more about the conspiracy. Anything we do to throw Jehan down might get us killed and break the peace between Terosalle and Lieda. I'm not willing to do that."

"So the conspirators get away with everything. Rule of all Feyndala. Youth and beauty they've already spent once and now have stolen from others. And more will die to feed that youth and to spread their influence. It's not fair. I want them broken, cast down, ruined. Killed."

"Are you willing to die to bring this about?"

"Yes."

"And our baby?"

"You bastard." She rolled over, drawing away from me.

"Are you willing to leave in the morning, get as far afield as possible, so I can cause some trouble here and then scamper off to join you?"

"No."

"Then what we're going to do is watch Thaliara and Buyan get married tomorrow, and smile and offer congratulations, and leave revenge to the gods."

"No."

I sighed in exasperation. "What do you recommend, then?"

"We expose the conspirators at the wedding and let their own allies drag them down to tear them to pieces."

"And how do we prove this conspiracy? Show them the chamber where they wrench spirits from their prisoners? That's a sort of magic none has seen before, else we'd have heard of it—in legend, anyway. It might take forever for them to understand the truth of our words. My guess is that we'd be assassinated well before our point was made."

She rolled back over against me. "You remember what Teuper was saying about all of them getting sick, the blow they felt?"

"Uhh . . . I think so."

"I'm certain that 'all of them' is all the people with spirits in them. You remember how ill Elowar looked when we went to conduct her to the meal."

"Yes."

"I'm just as certain that I know what made them sick."

She told me.

❖   ❖   ❖

At times during the night, I heard her humming and singing. Sometimes it was her notes to repel spirits, but she wove them together with musical bridges to make a wordless song of them. Sometimes it was the "Spring Hunting Song." And sometimes it was a tune that was hauntingly familiar. I listened to the words:

"Silver dancing, silver prancing/each the same as one before; silver diving, silver rising/each the same as one before. Clumsy stroke and redness welling/each the same as one before; mother, stop the girl from yelling/each the same as one before."

Nonsense lyrics. It took me a while to grasp their meaning. It was a Liedan child's sewing song, one I hadn't heard since I was little—something mothers absently sang to their daughters as they sat together patching clothes. It was well-suited to the idea she'd explained to me, and it was obvious she was flexing the muscles of her magical talent for the events of the day to come.

I thought about that. Spirit-magic was the province of mages, shaping magic more the province of Bards. Hers was more a pure mage's natural ability, yet shaped by the Bardic training she'd had at Shallia's hands. I wondered what this hybrid art would be—some failed branch of magical exploration, or a new form to which we could attach her name as discoverer?

In the midst of the night she awoke me. "I feel it," she said. "Spirit-magic. Not mine."

I rose. "From the caves."

"No." She pointed toward our door—toward the east, away from Jehan's hidden caves.

We dressed. Halleyne said she could point directly at the source of the magic she felt, and if her direction were true, it was outside in the open air—or perhaps on the top of the wall, or on the face of the eastern mountain.

We crept about in the halls until I found one with a mountain-man guard outside. "Do you know," I asked him, "which room belongs to Loneyt of the Rockfalls?"

He grimaced and pointed. "At the end, to the right."

We were in luck; that was one of the rooms facing east.

Loneyt, bleary-eyed and irritable, answered our second knock. His expression cleared as he recognized us.

"We need your window," I said.

"You have decided against Jehan?"

"That was never in doubt."

He admitted us. I told him not to light his lamp. Crossing toward the barely-visible window, Halleyne managed to stumble across the bed and fall onto it; there were two female squeaks.

"My lady, Ceauma of the Rockfalls."

"My apologies."

A woman's voice, new to me, in poor Terosai: "It is nothing."

I got to the window, pulled aside the drapes over it, and slowly pushed the shutters partway open. Moonlight spilled in. Halleyne joined me. Loneyt fell in behind her; after a few moments' rustling of bedclothes, his lady did too.

Halleyne pointed—just above the eastern citadel wall, where the roof of the barn that housed the box-winch rose above the wall heights. Barely visible atop the roof were two human silhouettes. "There. I can barely make it out." Her voice was a whisper.

"Give it time for your eyes to adjust to the darkness," I told her. "Looks like a man and a woman. She has a cloak on, but her hair bespeaks her sex."

"Maybe not," Loneyt said. "Many mountain clansmen wear their hair long."

"It is man and woman," Ceauma said. "He is naked."

I squinted. She was right; the man was nude, despite the altitude and cold.

"Remind you of something?" Halleyne asked.

"Teuper," I said. On Fishtail, we'd once found him standing nude, mindless, atop a hill in the coldest part of winter. He'd claimed not to know how he got there, but we later reasoned he'd been spirit-summoning, bargaining with the wind much as Halleyne had later done. But the spells as he knew them seemed to demand he be nude.

Halleyne gasped at nothing I could see, then said, "The wind comes."

She was right. A wind blew hard against the banners on the walls, against the shutters. I stopped them with my palms before they could crash shut and perhaps alert or awaken others. Through the gap still remaining I could see the woman's cloak billow up, see her hold something aloft.

A cylinder—no, a scroll. The wind took it and spun it round and round the two people, then sped it off into the night sky.

"The wind bears it away," Loneyt said. "Like a messenger?"

Halleyne said, "Precisely right. He's using the

very wind as his courier. See it speed to the east? My bet is it's going straight for some Terosai city."

"Don't bet with her," I told the Rockfalls.

The man atop the barn stooped, then straightened to whirl a cloak around himself. Both he and the woman descended somehow from their rooftop, disappearing from our sight.

"Why not south?" I wondered. "You'd think they'd want to send messages to the capital."

"The cities of dar Butha and dar Daini are eastern ports," Halleyne said. "If they were going to dispatch a ship to Landfall—"

"—to get to Lia first—"

"—those would be the closest ports. Then Thaliara could pretend to be as happy as a new heiress that her mother still lived, because her mother would be dead before reaching Feyndala again."

I cursed. Well, with luck, *Driftwood* was already long gone with her passengers.

"What does this have to do with Jehan?" asked the Rockfall chief.

"Nothing immediately," I told him. "So let me give you this gift instead. Sora is Jehan's daughter, Teuper's sister. If he told you he chose her on merit or to reward her for suffering at Red Lances captivity, he lied—a strike against his honor."

"Good." There was satisfaction in his voice. "This I can use."

We watched until the two rooftop figures walked into our sight again en route to the mansion. They were Thaliara and Teuper.

Chapter Thirteen

We thanked Loneyt and Ceauma and returned to our own chamber. "I have to reach Shallia's mind," Halleyne said.

"I thought you'd been reaching out for her every night. It hasn't worked so far."

"No. But I've been seeking Shallia's spirit. She is a normal woman in a world full of them. I know of another spirit near her, one far more distinctive." She looked troubled. "If I can find it, perhaps I can find her near it."

"You mean Snake-Mother."

"Yes. I haven't tried this before for fear of her. But if Shallia has still more enemies seeking her—"

"You're right."

This time, we did everything we could to improve Halleyne's chances, everything her limited magical training had taught her. We made a protective circle of candle drippings, wax into which she sang, again and again, the notes of her spell to repel unwanted spirits. She sat in the center of the circle and composed herself for a long time.

Then she sang her hunting song. It was not as she had sung it before; she changed the chords,

the tempo, the arrangement until it was a
mournful mockery of that gay love-seeking tune.
It actually became repellent to me and I knew
she was infusing it with what she remembered
of Snake-Mother's spirit. As like is attracted to
like, she wanted her song to find its way to Snake-
Mother's ear . . . or whatever a serpent goddess
used for ears.

Her voice became lower until I could barely
hear her. Then she ceased singing altogether. I
could not even tell if she were breathing, but did
not dare step through the circle for fear it might
interrupt her during the rapture of her spell.

That's when I noticed the gray men and women.
A dozen of them or more, all naked, they came
through the walls, the doors, the ceiling, floating
as if borne aloft by friendly winds. But their
expressions were not friendly. They ignored me
altogether, looking upon Halleyne with an expression something like lust, something like awe, and
reached for her—

I drew my knife and slashed at the nearest
man. The steel bit into the thin gossamer of his
being. He saw me for the first time, and, vexed
by my blow, floated away; a thin gray substance
flowed from the wound I'd put in his arm.

But another ten of them were still reaching.
Their hands stopped as if hitting a wall above the
place where the wax circle lay, and for a moment
I thought Halleyne protected. But I saw the wax
begin to chip away as though by unseen hands.

I laid into the gray spirits, slashing and cutting,
forcing them back, but I could only defend one
half the circle at a time; opposite, they always
clawed and reached. And always the wax became

thinner. I ran around the circle cutting as fast as I could, but they returned to harry the opposite side.

"Halleyne," I suggested, "please wake up."

She did not. But she moved—reached out, embracing nothing. Then the nothing became a shimmer of light and was suddenly transformed into Shallia's image. Shallia embraced Halleyne, the hug a clumsy one because their bodies overlapped and intersected in strange ways. The faces of the gray spirits lit up and they redoubled their efforts.

Halleyne and Shallia kept their eyes closed. They spoke to one another in silent words. In one of my passages around the circle I got my hands on the broadsword my sister had given me, and was able to sweep it through three and four spirits at a time; this, at last, began to keep them all at bay. They floated back to stay clear of the steel. But I was getting tired.

Shallia and my lady embraced again. Halleyne held up her hand and quietly sang the notes that would send spirits packing. Shallia vanished as though she were made of air, and the gray spirits also fled, some slapping into walls and doors, some merely fading away as Shallia had done.

I set the sword down and sank panting into the chair.

Halleyne opened her eyes. "I reached her mind—Kin! You're sweating. What have you been doing?"

"Nothing," I said. "It just tires me to watch you work."

She told me that *Driftwood* and *Byriver* were still

at anchor. Something had been decided between their captains and they were soon to sail. But Snake-Mother was awake and they had to move. This was the little Halleyne had been able to understand from Shallia's thoughts. She did not know whether Shallia understood her about the possibility of a Terosai ship hunting them. And the uncertainty of it all ate at Halleyne, keeping her sleepless in my arms through the remainder of that long night.

Well before dawn, I heard the bustle begin: servants rustling through the hallways, cleaning, awakening the nobles who'd wished to rise early.

Just before dawn, a knock sounded on our own door.

I opened it. Outside stood Elowar. The muscles of her face were tight, restraining, I thought, an expression of pain or grief. Behind her were General Oakwall and the mage Burslan. I admitted them.

"I awoke you," she said.

"No." I turned up the table lamp to illuminate the room.

"You . . ." She could not speak for a long moment. "You were right."

"About Sheroit?"

"He came to me late. Told me we each needed the same thing. To spend years in our respective domains, building them, managing them. We could not divide our time between Bontiniard and Marketry. He could not wed me. When he left, I told one of my ladies to gossip about the succession of Lieda. And then, scarce an hour ago, Sheroit came again to my chambers . . . full of mad passion, as you said. Repentant. Agonized by the mistake he'd made. He said he'd abandon his own nation to be with me."

"What did you tell him?"

"I said I loved him more than life itself, and sent him away happy." She gave me a faint smile that was without joy. "Judges and negotiators are not the only ones skilled at lying.

"Kin, Halleyne, I will have revenge. But I want whatever sword I have to sink deep, and I'm sure you know how to sink it. I have never said this before, to anyone: command me."

"Take your retinue and leave. You can be half a day's ride away before the wedding starts."

She shook her head, smiling sadly. "I'm still a princess. I can refuse commands that do not suit me."

"Then consign your spirit to the gods, because, like Halleyne and me, you will probably be dead before nightfall."

At midmorning, the assembly began gathering in the great hall. The tables had been cleared away; they were now in the courtyard outside, gathering snow, but would be brought back in for the feast afterwards. Except I knew the only feast would be for carrion-birds.

The benches were pressed into service as seating in the hall, but most of those present preferred to stand until the event; they clustered along national and clan lines in small groups, planning, politicking. Naturally, the bride and groom were not yet to be seen.

I talked a few minutes with Baron Loneyt of the Rockfalls. When I returned to Halleyne's side, I noted with satisfaction the growing number of Liedan guardsmen, wearing their finest nonuniform dress, scattered throughout the hall. An event of this sort precluded the wearing of any arm other than a knife—unless one was a Guardsman, the role Viriat and Jenina had assumed at my own wedding. But I suspected that there would be many, many knives at hand today. In spite of the fact that I was sweating constantly, I was happy to be wearing the chain mail my sister had given me under my overtunic. With luck, no glad-handing courtier would clap me on the back and detect its presence.

The hall filled. King Jehan arrived with Teuper, Sora, and his retinue. Elowar stood with her own retinue and Sheroit was with her, offering her dainty morsels from the platters of servants, smiling down at her with the solicitousness of a lover.

Another retinue, this time of an old, old woman in extremely rich Terosai dress, carrying and supporting herself on a gilt staff with a curiously lumpy gold head. Halleyne clutched my hand. "Senior priestess of the All-Mother. From our capital. I'm surprised she had the strength to make this voyage . . . but it's appropriate that it be her to perform such an important marriage."

"What's that on her staff?"

"A statuette of the All-Mother. In a very old artistic style. She is shown with huge belly and breasts and hips, no head, little stumps for arms and legs . . ."

"All the attributes of fertility, with nought else being important."

"Something like that."

King Jehan, alerted by some signal I did not see, moved up to his throne and raised his hand

for the crowd's attention. The noise abated a little.
"Lords and Ladies—or perhaps I should say
Ladies and Lords, to be in keeping with Terosai
custom—please sit and make ready. The grand
moment is upon us." There was bit of applause;
Jehan bowed to the aged priestess and moved
aside that she might take his place. She did,
moving with studied elegance, and turned to smile
out over the audience.

There was a great shuffling among the onlookers, with Liedans moving to the left bank of
benches in the hall, Terosai moving to the right,
and the mountain clansmen sitting wherever they
chose; it was as though the priestess had cast a
spell to part the waves.

I saw many in the crowd turning back to look
at the entrance of the hall. I followed suit.
Captain—*General*—Buyan stood at the door in
the flowing robes of Terosai noblemen, all in light
blues and black, a striking figure. Behind him was
a uniformed Terosai soldier, a captain by his marks
of rank, a large man with a huge two-handed
sword carried across his back. I took special note
of him; he would probably be trying to kill me
in a very few minutes.

Then Buyan was joined by his bride-to-be.
Queen Thaliara wore a gown of iridescent blue,
a form-fitting Liedan design that set off her
youthful figure to good advantage; there was a
murmur of appreciation from the crowd. Behind
her stood another captain, identical in dress and
armament to Buyan's; in fact, as I peered closer,
I could see that the two men were identical in
every way. Twins. That cheered me a little;
perhaps they'd been chosen more for their visual

attributes than fighting ability. But then, someone as powerful as Thaliara could doubtless choose for both traits.

The there were three hollow booms from the thronal portion of the room, the aged priestess hammering the stone floor with her staff. Then, in a clear and melodious voice, she called, "In the name of she who is mother of us all, I compel you, Thaliara, Gloriana Majeste of Terosalle, Most High Tarrene of the Realm, come forward."

The queen did so, moving easily, betraying no nervousness, until she and her Guardsman stood before the priestess.

"I compel you, Doniar Buyan, General of the Armies of Terosalle, come forward."

He did so, a small smile of satisfaction on his lips. I could see no tenderness there, just appreciation of the moment—perhaps appreciation of his own wonderfulness.

"We are here," the priestess said, "in clear view of the goddess, that she might smile down upon us and bless the happy celebrants with her mercy, her fruitfulness, and her kind regard. Nor is this merely a union of lovers but of nations, a living symbol of the end of warfare and the resumption of alliance."

I felt that statement was ironic enough to serve as my cue. I stood on my bench and shouted "Challenge!"

Everyone in the hall, groom and bride included, turned to look at me. Most had expressions of blank surprise; some were already graduating into anger. I felt a moment of irrational dismay, the realization that I'd just done something so vile that my father must surely materialize out of nowhere and give me the beating of my life. "Challenge!" I repeated. "This wedding cannot be." I hopped down again, then side-stepped until I was in the aisle between ranks of benches.

"Shut up and sit down, Underbridge." That was King Jehan, seated at the front rank of the audience, his face suggesting my interruption had put him in a dangerous mood.

"It is for me to speak," said the priestess. "Mine is the authority here." She turned back to me. "Am I to understand that you challenge Buyan for the right to wed Thaliara?"

"No!" I affected a look of shock. "What use would I have for that treacherous royal baggage?"

Gasps, a sudden rise in conversation, a few chuckles. Thaliara's face became so angry it finally reminded me of her mother's. Buyan stepped forward but Jehan rose and restrained him. People around me were standing; those behind them had to stand too in order to see.

"No," I continued, "I challenge this because it is unlawful. I will explain. Buyan, since his release from imaginary captivity, has not renounced his oaths to Lieda; he is still a citizen of my nation. I, as Judge of Lieda, pronounce him guilty of crimes of conspiracy against the Crown and declare him a prisoner of my office. As a convicted criminal now under the thumb of the Crown, he can't marry without permission." I shrugged to indicate the reasonableness of my position.

The noise from the crowd became louder: words of incredulity mostly, some of admiration from mountain clansmen only half-committed to King Jehan. My dread of being embarrassed was fading;

this experience was actually quite liberating. A pity
that my dread of being killed wasn't going away.

Finally Buyan found his voice. "I accept the
challenge. Captain, kill him." His Guardsman
approached me, bringing his great two-handed
sword up out of the rings that held it to his back;
the blade sang as it came free. He held it before
him as he advanced.

"Wait!" I called. "You haven't heard my Accusation yet."

This was an appeal to the priestess, to ancient
marriage traditions that were the same between
Terosalle and Lieda. She nodded and said, "Wait."

"Kill him," said Buyan.

"I command you to hear the Accusation," said
the priestess.

The Guardsman halted, unsure. Buyan might
have enough power to ruin or end his life; the
priestess could strike harder, recommending to the
very gods that he suffer more once his life was
over. I smiled at him. "Put the sword down," I
told him, "you'll need the rest." By challenging
his pride, I guaranteed that he would be forced
to hold it at the ready all the while I spoke.

"Now, my Accusation. Perhaps you should serve
some of the sweets and flavors you were holding
for the meal; I'm going to be at this awhile. King
Jehan, this Accusation starts with you. Your arrival
in Feyndala some thirteen, fifteen years ago?"

Jehan didn't respond.

"Call it fifteen. With your children. Teuper and
Sora."

Whispers from the audience: "Sora is his get?"

"Were they the only two? Or did you have more
children?"

Jehan thought about it, looking amongst the faces in the crowd. Then, "Only those two."

More murmurs. I felt good. I'd already wrung an admission from him.

"Well, then. Two talented children, strong in spirit-magic. Very innovative. The Black Rocks took you in. After a while, you killed their chief and took his mantle. All very legal, by mountain-clan standards.

"Then Captain Buyan and Prince Jernin visited Terosalle on a state visit. The Princess Thaliara saw these two sons of King Jerno and liked what was before her. Perhaps her admiration for Jernin was real; the minstrels certainly sang of it convincingly enough. But it was really Buyan who appealed more to her, probably his ambition, which matched hers. And this did not elude the attention of clever eyes—such as those of Sheroit dar Bontine, already one of the premier negotiators of all Feyndala, for all his lowly birth among the Black Rocks." I pointed to Sheroit, who stood beside Elowar.

He shrugged eloquently. "There is no shame in lowly birth. Only in staying lowly."

"What a well-spoken assassin you are. So the conspiracy was born. Sheroit and Jehan sending messengers to one another. Whispering into the ears of Thaliara and Buyan. 'You can each rule the nation of your parent. You can have one another. Between you, the entire continent can be yours.' But there were problems. Queen Lia could live a long time. King Jerno had three others sons—legitimate heirs, all.

"So you let yourselves be kidnapped by the Red Lances."

"Lies," Thaliara hissed. "Thirteen years we spent in bondage—"

"Any bondage you endured, Princess, was due to your own wishes and tastes," I told her. "This mysterious chieftain, Cenpeydon, your brutal captor? You know well that he did not die here moons ago, but that he stands beside you now. *Buyan* was Cenpeydon, his choice of name clear sign of the identity it hid."

The veins stood out on Buyan's neck. "I have had enough. Kill him now."

"Stand still," said the priestess, "or earn the wrath of my order."

The Guardsman flinched, torn between his two masters, but did not move. I could see his arms twitching a bit as he held the sword at the ready.

"Two nations at war. Other conspirators climbing the ranks of both courts through attrition. Minister Gastin in Lieda, who knows who all in Terosalle? The rulers ineffectual. The heirs dying one by one—all but Buyan and Thaliara, safe in the mountains. Jehan pulling strings out in the lowland nations while adding clan after clan to his little empire. And then the breakthroughs, the discovery of spirit-magics that would make the difference. Winds to blow two of the surviving rulers to their deaths . . . had not an island chain intervened. And spirit-rending magics to rip the very essences out of victims and give them to others, making them younger, concealing blemishes, granting strength—what other traits come with that magical drink all you chiefs imbibed?" I saw many of the clansmen looking to their chieftains and chieftainesses, sudden outbreaks of conversation and head-shaking among them.

Jehan's expression had gone from stages of disbelief and anger to evaluation and, now, calmness. I didn't like that.

"With Lia and Jerno dead and Elowar tempted by your promises of youth, a switch in tactics. Pieces moved around on the game board. Sheroit could wed Elowar, putting Lieda under direct Black Rock control. Buyan—discarded. You tell him he can still marry Thaliara, rule a mighty nation with her. But indirect control lies with King Jehan still; he controls the process of youthening, a process Thaliara has partaken of long before she needed to. Vain as her mother, and just as desperate."

I saw a dim light of realization ignite in Buyan's eye. He glanced aside at Jehan, who was ignoring him.

Jehan stood and moved around to face me. "Part of what this oaf says is true," he told the crowd. "Of course, he mixes lies with truth to baffle you. However, through my daughter Sora, wise beyond her years, I do control the very magic he describes. I can grant youth. Many of you chiefs have partaken of it. Every chief who has sworn himself to me may do so now: I grant this blessing to all who rule under me. And, yes, it comes at the expense of life—for the deaths of lawfully-convicted criminals fuels the process. Is there any among you who would turn down an offer of youth on such grounds?"

Someone cried "No!" from the back of the crowd. The cry was taken up by others. One aging red-beard stood and shouted, "I have sworn, I want to take my reward! Need you more criminals? I will bring you more!"

Jehan gave me an indulgent look. "I think you have misjudged your audience. No one here shares your sense of shock, Kin." He looked out over the crowd. "We will demonstrate the process of youthening. Drag down Kin Underbridge and I will grant his youthfulness to the most deserving among you."

Chapter Fourteen

A score or more wedding guests surged toward me, hands reaching. Then there was a wall between them and me, Liedan royal guards, daggers already out. The crowd stopped and its line began to change, some members withdrawing, others advancing, and benches clattered as they were knocked over. I heard the priestess shouting, trying to regain control, but none heeded her.

I took something from my belt pouch and held it aloft: a necklace of gold, from it dangling a locket. " 'To my daughter,' " I shouted, " 'on the occasion of her first kill, welcoming her to full womanhood.' Whose is it?"

One of the mountain chiefs struggling to reach me drew up short and looked as though I'd slapped him. "My daughter—she ran off with her lover—"

I had no time for explanations, for sympathy. I just threw him the jewelry. "I found it on a girl's corpse where Jehan hides the victims of his spirit-stealing magic. I'll bet she was no lawfully convicted criminal." I held up a gold ring. "A signet ring, ruby stone with a serpent hammered into it in fine gold wire?"

Another shocked face, another hand going up. I threw the woman the ring and held up one more piece of jewelry I'd pilfered from the bodies in the bags. "A cloak-clasp of a harp, rubies and emeralds—"

I got no further. A collective groan went up from the mountain clansmen. Whomever that dead man had been, he had been important to more than one clan. I hurled the brooch to the first hand to go up.

Then the scene, like some tapestry suspended between two ships sailing in opposite directions, rent and tore asunder.

I saw Jehan backhand the Terosai priestess without looking at her. She went down hard, badly hurt at the very least, perhaps slain. There was no way for him to survive such an offense committed against a high priestess . . . unless he killed every witness to it who was not loyal to him.

Buyan was in motion, striding toward me. He tore the greatsword from the hands of his Guardsman and shoved the man aside. The Guardsman literally flew into the crowd, knocking men and women down like bowling pins. I knew then that, like Gastin, he had received unholy strength from the spirit-magic, and I was more glad of it than I can relate.

I gestured and the Liedan royal guards around me stood back and away.

"A man of many words," Buyan said. "What are your final ones?" He raised the sword in one hand, whipping it about as lightly as if it were a modern rapier.

"Just these," I said. "I'm going to have my wife beat you up."

Halleyne stepped out of the circle around me and sang out the opening chords of the spirit-repelling song.

The song hit Buyan like a flight of arrows from a unit of champion archers. He staggered back and dropped the sword; it rang louder than the cries of the crowd. Others in the audience began shrieking, scrambling to get away from her; I saw several fall to the pavestones and empty their stomachs. Queen Thaliara was among them.

But it was Buyan she directed her song against, Buyan who felt the full force of her anger . . . and as I watched, something crawled out of him. A full-sized man, gray and indistinct, emerged from his flesh, pulling free as slowly as if they were adhered together. He was a mountain clansman, naked, face distorted in rage as he turned against Buyan.

Halleyne waved at the spirit and he flew away with her motion. His path took him straight into the fireplace, where he disappeared . . . and another gray form, this time a woman, began to emerge from Buyan's body. Buyan sank to his knees, his face growing dark with sickness.

As I bent to retrieve his sword, I saw motion from the corner of my eye—Sheroit dar Bontine lunging at my wife from behind. I whipped around to interpose myself. . . . Too late.

For he stopped before he could reach Halleyne. His eyes widened as he bent over backwards, clawing at his back. His knees gave way and I could finally see the blood pouring from his spine.

Blood matching that on the knife in Elowar's hands. The former queen, to judge from her pallor and stooping posture, was as sick as any spirit-infested member of this horrible crowd, but I saw determination in her eyes that surpassed theirs. She plunged the knife into his back twice more and let him fall. Then she, too, swayed, into the arms of one of her bodyguards.

Halleyne spun slowly in place, her face distorted with the effort she was putting into her song. As she turned, more in the crowd suffered the full effects of her magic. Spirits tore free from the men and women carrying them. I saw a middle-aged man go old before my eyes, withering, muscle shrinking from his arms and legs, hair going from gray-brown to pure gray to white and wispy. He clutched his chest and fell motionless, his eyes staring forever into the floor's stones.

And every one of those spirits turned to grasp at its former owner, but Halleyne waved each away to fly into the central fireplace.

I handed off the greatsword to one of Elowar's guards. Not my choice of weapon, too big and clumsy for such tight quarters. I drew my short sword and dagger from beneath my cloak and stepped before a gold-bedecked mountain chieftain lunging at Halleyne. I parried his dagger with my own and opened up his gut with the short sword. He staggered away, shocked and dying.

Where were the royals? I saw Jehan and Sora, unaffected by Halleyne's song, carrying Teuper between them around the fringes of the crowd. Thaliara, obviously ill, followed them. She still looked seventeen; Halleyne had obviously not yet hit her with the magic of her song.

Then it happened. A gray girl-spirit, beautiful but savagely angry, ripped its way out of Thaliara. I saw the Terosai queen's face change, losing no beauty but gaining a little character, some lines around the eyes. The agony of the separation was too great for her; she curled into a ball as she fell.

I tried to make sense of what was happening. Mountain clansmen fought with one another. Jehan's guards clashed with clansmen, with Liedan guards. I saw archers appear on the balcony above the throne, the balcony that was normally for guests. They brought bows to bear but, before they could fire, they died one after the other, their backs and throats rent by the knives of Liedan guardsmen Elowar had stationed up there.

Mountain clansmen joined us. Chief Loneyt of the Rockfalls and his lady Ceauma, tears in their garments exposing armor they'd worn to this happy occasion. Two clansmen to whom I'd given the jewelry of their slain loved ones stood among us; their followers joined us against Jehan's minions.

I saw Burslan complete a complicated series of motions and passes. Suddenly a number of men and women in the hall shrieked, fell to the floor, tearing at their clothes, dropping their weapons.

But the numbers of the enemy were still too great, ours too few. With the motion of a storm-tossed bay, the sea of people in the hall separated into two armed camps: mine, at the center, knives pointed out; theirs, three times as numerous, all around, knives pointed in. More men and women, armed and sometimes armored, were charging in from the doors . . . and joining Jehan's force.

A few more clashes of blades, then a moment's respite. The only sounds were the moans of the injured and sick.

I spared a glance for Elowar. She was unconscious, or nearly so, in her bodyguard's arms. She was still young. Halleyne had spared her.

Jehan, from beside the fireplace, shouted, "It's over. You can see your position is impossible."

"Turn on Jehan!" I cried. "Or he will steal away your loved ones and grind them into the paste of youth."

One solitary member of the ring around us, a young mountain woman with paired knives, spun around and backed into our line.

Jehan smiled. "You're a failure as a recruiter, Kin."

Halleyne began singing again, more softly this time, directly toward Jehan: "Silver dancing, silver prancing/each the same as one before; silver diving, silver rising/each the same as one before."

Jehan continued, "And your wife has gone mad."

"Clumsy stroke and redness welling/each the same as one before; mother, stop the girl from yelling/each the same as one before."

"Would you shut her up?"

"Turn on Teuper," I cried. "When Jehan dies, Teuper will be your king . . . guilty of three dishonors."

There was more muttering in the crowd. Then a black-haired chieftainess walked through threatening knives into our midst and turned to face her former allies. Her followers streamed in behind her. One of them carried the body of the Terosai priestess. The chieftainess glared at Jehan and Teuper.

The big red-haired chief who had shouted so approvingly of stolen youth followed suit. Our numbers began to swell, and I saw Jehan's face change as he sensed the tide turning against him.

"I disown Teuper," he said, and his son turned a sick, betrayed face up to stare at his father. Jehan ignored him and raised a hand on high: "Which of you still loyal will be my new heir? We will decide when all their heads are on spears."

Halleyne, incongruously, still sang from our midst, lyrics of pulling thread and flying colors, valiant thimbles, perfect hems.

There still weren't enough of us to win this day. I turned to catch General Oakwall's eye. "The doors," I said.

There was a heavy blow against the stone of the fireplace behind Jehan. Puzzled, the king turned to look. Half the people in the hall looked.

Another blow. It sounded as though a siege engine, a ram, had struck the stones beside the fireplace.

From the far side.

There was a third blow and a portion of the stone wall, a yard in diameter, gave way, spilling stones across King Jehan's feet. And something crawled through to stand beside him.

It was a dead man, eyes shriveled but not rotted, skin brown and wrinkled as though with age, clothes gaily festive, as if mocking both his death and the wedding garments of the guests all around. It turned and stumbled toward Sora.

King Jehan grabbed it around the neck. "Kill it!"

But the corpse was stronger than Jehan. It reached up and yanked his grip free, tossed him negligently aside, into the crowd.

Another dead man crawled through the hole and stood.

Men and women shrieked, drew away from the

new arrivals. A guardsman loyal to Jehan charged the first marching corpse, thrust his sword into its innards. The blow parted flesh, the sword emerged from the thing's back, but the dead man was not inconvenienced. He marched on toward the retreating Sora, arms outstretched, driving the guardsman on before it. Sora shrieked.

I bent to speak into Halleyne's ear. "Many?" I asked. *Are there many more to come?*

She shook her head but kept singing, using her sewing-song as her focus of concentration, stitching the spirits of the dead back to their bodies in a cruel simulation of life. A condition she had said would be temporary if she could manage it at all.

I caught General Oakwall's eye and said, "Now."

He nodded, turned toward the exit from the great hall. "Lieda departs!" he shouted, and the guardsmen on that side renewed the fight.

"Come, you legions of the dead!" I cried. "Come in your teeming thousands and slaughter all who hold faith with Jehan!"

A dead woman emerged from the hole and a dead man came after her. So far my "teeming thousands" were only five, but our enemies did not know that. The last three dead intruders stumbled into the crowd, perhaps seeking those who once had contained their unwilling spirits.

But the horror of those dead faces was too much for many of Jehan's defenders. The crowd parted before the walking dead. Those who were brave enough to stand ground and stab away were brushed aside by nerveless arms. Some in the crowd shouted names in tones of dismay as they recognized the clothes once worn by loved ones now lost, and a few more mountain clansmen joined our circle.

We lurched into motion, the entire weapon circle of us moving toward the door. The line between us and it was thinner, many of Jehan's faithful having shifted around to protect Sora. General Oakwall gave a sudden yell and his side of the circle charged forward, stabbing, striking, and the line before him gave way. I, on the other side, backed up as fast as I could, striking against those who came too close, parrying knife-blows as fast as they came.

Suddenly we were out in the foyer. Back in the great hall I could see more dead crawling from the chimney, Jehan's followers too full of dread to make a stand at the hole and prevent more from emerging. I heard the snap of bowstrings and saw Liedan archers on the stairways to the upper floors; they were making a staged descent, one running a few steps and then firing, the next passing him by and doing the same, using bows they'd taken from Jehan's archers on the balconies. Their arrow fire melted away part of the line facing us and they joined us.

Our swelling force made it out to the courtyard and the snowfall. There seemed to be hundreds of soldiers and clansmen shouting and running out there, and fighting was already going on at the gates: more of General Oakwall's uniformed force was guarding the gate, keeping it open. We surged in that direction.

The forces harrying us from the rear were reinforced by latecomers. Jehan's guards, armed with sword and spear, longer weapons than we had. Among them was Buyan, a patch of vomit still clinging to his cheek, a Liedan cavalry saber in his hand, and as their force reached ours he angled over to come after me.

He offered no words this time. He brought down the saber at me, a fast, hard overhand blow. I brought up both dagger and short sword crossed at the hilts and caught the blade in the "X" they made. Had he still carried the strength of many spirits, he would have cleaved through my parry, but I stopped his blow.

I kicked at his groin. He twisted away from my move, continued his turn so that his back was to me, whipped around to face me again . . . and the saber angled in toward my side, a barely-seen blur, the force of his spin moving it at deadly speed.

I made no effort to block it. The sharp, light blade bit at my side just under my arm. There was a faint metallic noise and it stopped there, tearing my tunic but nothing beneath.

I clamped my dagger-arm down over the blade, dropped the dagger, grabbed his sword hilt with that hand. "You're no longer strong enough to shatter chain mail," I said. His face registered surprise and I drove my short sword into him.

He folded up over it, grabbing at me. I let him keep the short sword and took his saber with me as I backed away. An even trade of weapons, an unfair deal when all the blood was counted in.

A number of the guardsmen stayed with him, surrounding him, protecting him from further harm. I saw light fade from his eyes and doubted any healing mage could get to him in time. Other attackers, sensing their numbers diminishing, hung back. In moments we at the rear were able to turn tail and flee.

We made the wall-gate with no further loss. Beyond, the barn where the great winch operated the lift was already in Liedan hands. Mountain clan guards lay here and there, blood still flowing freshly from their wounds.

Someone with heroic aspirations would have been embarrassed to be among the first into the box. Me, I was grateful. I held my wife, steadied the guardsman carrying Elowar. More of her retinue was loaded aboard. So was the man carrying the aged Terosai priestess.

General Oakwall didn't join us. "I'll be down straightway," he said. "We have to hold here until a load or two have reached the ground."

I saluted him with the saber, then gave it to him. I could think of nothing to say. I doubted I would ever see him alive. There was a lurch and the box began its descent.

Below, the encampments were active as anthills; a thick crowd of onlookers of all three nations waited as we descended.

The cold air revived Elowar. She stiffly thanked her bodyguard and insisted that she be put down. She looked at the backs of her hands and gave Halleyne a look that was half gratitude, half worry.

The priestess, too, was alive; I heard her moan.

I caught Burslan's eye. "What did you do to them in the hall?"

"You know I can drive ticks and lice to a frenzy of fear so they will leave our bedclothes alone."

"Yes?"

He looked quite satisfied. "I can also drive them to a frenzy of hunger. A little thing I do. Some of those mountain folk are, well, not adequately groomed."

"What has happened?" called the onlookers from below.

"Steady us!" I shouted. "And arm yourselves! Cenpeydon's brother has come for revenge!"

Cenpeydon, the magical name. Most of them scattered to reach their loved ones and their weapons. None helped steady the car as it came to a too-sudden stop against the ground. We piled out over the rail, none waiting for the little door to open. Burslan and I both gave rising-fist signs to the watchers overhead and the box started up again.

We charged back to the Liedan camp, others among us taking up the "Cenpeydon's brother!" cry.

The queen's ladies-in-waiting, dispatched earlier, were already among our tents. They could not saddle our horses, of course; such untoward activity would have alerted those in the other camps. But they'd packed as much of our supplies and clothing as they could without being obvious.

At our picket line, each of us saddled his own horse, then one other, as we watched the box ascend and begin a second descent with a too-heavy load of guardsmen.

"How long can they hold?" the queen asked. She was saddling a third horse, her skill and experience with the animals making her faster than most of the rest of us despite her illness.

"Not long," I said. "Wooden building, big doors. I'll be surprised if another load makes it."

She mounted her horse; it danced around a bit, agitated by the noise and excitement. The second load touched down and soldiers spilled over the rail, running toward us; mountain men also emerged, and a big, shaggy one, Loneyt, gave us a celebratory wave and yell before running for his own camp with his wife. The box ascended once more.

There were soldiers atop the citadel walls now. They bellowed down at the crowds, pointing to us, but the crowd's shouted questions about Cenpeydon's imaginary brother drowned out the orders they wished to give. A couple of archers on the walls opened fire on us; we began to withdraw, leaving our tents and unpacked possessions behind.

The second batch of guards, twenty or so, joined us. The box reached the summit again. I mounted my horse and drew Halleyne up before me; her gaze did not waver from the underside of the citadel.

The box began another descent. When it was a third of the way down a Liedan soldier fell into it from above, a rooster-trail of blood streaming from his neck.

A quarter of the way from the ground, ten or more paces up in the air, it stopped . . . then began to ascend. The soldiers in it looked up, then began going over the sides, taking the consequences of the long drop in preference to the consequence of a return to the citadel.

Then I saw the figure. Someone was near the top of one of the ropes, holding on there as if for dear life. I could see from build and hair color that it was General Oakwall. He held on with one hand, motioning in a way I didn't recognize with the other. "What's he doing?" I asked.

There was pain in Halleyne's voice. "Sawing."

I saw him struck in the leg by an arrow from almost immediately above. He swayed, almost let go, but returned to his cutting.

Then the rope gave way. He fell, flailing, and smashed into the stones below. I saw blood all over the boulder his head struck. The box swayed on three ropes.

There was still someone in it, a woman, also sawing. I saw the second rope give and the box tipped over, swinging toward the east face of the mountain. The Liedan guardswoman managed to hold onto the rail and dropped from it when the box began its return swing. Her fall, so much shorter than Oakwall's, was not fatal; I saw her hit, saw her stand on one good leg, saw another Liedan reach her and bear her toward us.

More than a hundred and fifty of us had entered the citadel of Mount Rozinki; only two-thirds that number reached the encampment to flee. We were not joined by the mountain clansmen who'd sided with us; they could take to backtrails our horses could never follow, and did.

We galloped northward on the straightaways, traveled as fast as we could on the much more numerous rough portions of the trail. Still, we didn't make good time. Most of the ladies-in-waiting were doubled up on horses behind better riders, weighing down horses that were better suited to flatlands.

I trotted up alongside the black-haired mountain woman who'd cut the second line. Burslan said her leg was broken; he'd have to attend it with his magics when she could be still for some hours. She gave little sign of pain as she rode her mountain pony. "Will they catch us?" I asked.

She nodded. "Once they get down, they'll pursue with beasts like Clover here." She smacked her mount's neck with affection. "Hardier than these damned Liedan racing horses. One day, two days, they'll be on us."

I dropped back. "Gods, this is familiar. But the last time I did it, we were on foot."

"With engineers," Halleyne said.

"Yes. I remember some of their tricks. Perhaps I could do some of what they did . . . deadfalls, false snares to worry our pursuers . . ."

She gave me a bitter little smile. "As long as you remember that I'll be there with you, hauling rocks and stringing ropes."

"Perhaps I'll just ride hard."

"Good choice."

Chapter Fifteen

They didn't catch up to us that first day. But when darkness and exhaustion claimed us and we made camp, we could see their campfires in the distance behind. The night was so clear we could almost see individual figures against their fires. They would be upon us sometime tomorrow.

Elowar, subdued, joined Halleyne and me as we huddled around one of our own fires. "You left me my youth," she said. "Stolen youth, with lives lost to give it to me."

Halleyne paused to consider her words. "Those lives are already lost, Majesty. Highness. No one would benefit if I wrenched them out of you."

"I would. I want you to do so. I saw the looks in the eyes of those spirits as you yanked them free; hatred, beyond anything I can recall, for the men and women who carried them."

"If she does so," I said, "you will become frailer. Unable to withstand the rigors of this trip. You'll probably die."

Elowar shrugged.

Halleyne said, "You should know that the spirits hated their hosts not because they were trapped. It was because they knew the natures of those

244

they inhabited. Yours know your nature, too, and are not full of hate and spite. This is because of what you are."

The former queen looked surprised. "They are . . . content?"

"They are."

Elowar thought about that for a time, then left us to make her bed.

"That was quite a story," I said mildly.

"A lie, you mean."

"Well . . . when I say 'lie' I do not always imply criticism."

She managed a faint smile, but it did not conceal the fact that she was half-sick with guilt. "Kin, she has lost everything. Is it wrong to leave her this, a second life?"

"I don't know. I hope not. Halleyne?"

"Yes?"

"In all that has happened today, I know that I've forgotten to say how very proud I am of you. You turned tragedy into . . . survival."

Her eyes shone. "Is that all?"

"No. I love you."

"Good. Then you don't have to sleep in the snow."

Two of our wounded died during that night, despite the efforts of Burslan and soldiers trained in true medicine to save them. The priestess was not among them; she regained consciousness by morning. But early the next morning, an unhurt cavalry lieutenant was pitched from his horse on a rough stretch of road and died of a broken neck. Still we rode on, and whenever we could look back across a long stretch of roadway or river bed, we saw the pursuing force of horsemen, closer than they had been before.

"I'll say this, husband. You've given me a memorable wedding tour."

"I'll marry you again and give you a better one next time."

By midday they were only a few hundred paces back, slowly gaining. We were on a rise heading to a cleft between two hills. On the far side the land descended and broadened into a long stretch of mountain pasturage.

"When we reach the pastures," Elowar said, "they'll catch up to us. That will be the end."

Halleyne, holding on to me from behind, said, "We can try to hold that little pass ahead."

Elowar gave her a glum nod. "I'll ask for a volunteer force. If they hold long enough . . ." She trotted on ahead. I assumed she would reach the vanguard of our force and begin asking for volunteers; they could drop back to the rear as we traveled.

But I didn't have much hope. The cleft was merely the swiftest way into the pastures beyond. There were many trails on this part of Black Rock Road, trails used by goatherds and shepherds. An hour, two hours, and the pursuers would be around behind our volunteers.

Mere minutes later I heard shouts from ahead. Cries of alarm. And my heart sank. I knew at once what had happened; Jehan had dispatched fast riders along other mountain trails, ones which appeared on no map known to flatlanders. Some of his force was already ahead of us, waiting in the pastures. We were trapped between two pincers of a force that would kill us.

The riders ahead began calling "Underbridge! Underbridge!" I spurred my horse on to as fast a pace as I dared, passing other riders where the road was wide enough. Ahead, riders were slowing.

"Underbridge!"

I neared the cleft, just a broad dip between two rises of icy granite. A little further and Halleyne and I would be able to see down into the pasturage. The only riders ahead of me now were Elowar and Burslan, and it was the princess calling my name. I drew abreast of her.

No, it was not *my* name she was calling.

She stared down into the pastures at the cavalry force headed straight for us. They were even closer than our pursuers. Two or three hundred hard-riding men and women, all of them on mountain ponies. Elowar beamed down at them.

The banner-bearers carried the flag of Lieda and the flag of the Liedan Fifth Cavalry—the Black Chargers, a unit I well knew from my youth.

Elowar called, "Underbridge!" again and waved down at my father, who rode at the head of the force.

We drew aside as they came abreast of us. Father waved his captain on.

"Pursuit?" he asked.

"About two hundred," Elowar said. "Mountain riders."

"Are they tired?"

"They should be. We've led them a merry chase."

He grinned like a wolf. I hadn't seen him do that in some time. "We're not."

Rider after rider passed us. Archers. Lancers. Jehan's force would do well to turn and run. If his commander were smart enough, that's just what they'd do.

"How are you here?" I asked.

He shrugged. "The king. When he resumed his throne, he restored my rank and sent me down to conduct a new ambassador to Mount Rozinki . . . and to see if we could aid you. We made good time to get to you. No carriages to slow us down. Killed some good horses to do it. Good to see you again, son, daughter."

I could hear the smile in Halleyne's voice. "Better to see you."

He looked beyond us, to the south. "I take it there will be no need for an ambassador."

"Not for some time," I said. "Father?"

"Yes?"

"Once upon a time, when you arranged my appointment as Prince Balaquin's companion, I was embarrassed. Angry that you'd wield the mighty general's rank to keep me safe when the other lads had to march off to war. And now you've rushed off to my rescue again."

He snorted, amused. "And?"

"This time, I'm not angry." I spurred my horse. As we passed him, I said, "Don't fight if you don't have to. And, Father?"

"Yes?"

I called back to him over my shoulder. "I hope you weren't too happy with your retirement. If we're not at war now, we will be soon."

With our reinforcements, we outnumbered Jehan's men badly—badly enough that we engaged only briefly, as the leading edge of his troops caught up with the first of our reinforcements. Then his men broke off and fled back the way they had come.

We did not pursue—we could not hope for an advantage when every step moved them closer to home and us further from it, when every extra hour that we spent among the mountains would give Jehan opportunities to send assassins along back pathways to waylay us, or topple stones or spells down on our heads.

Instead, we returned home by a route as arduous as the one that had brought us to Jehan's citadel, at the fastest pace we could manage. We spread our news along the way—the tales of Jehan's evil, of dar Bontine's treachery, of Teuper's shame—and everywhere we went, we picked up supporters and followers and allies, and when we marched into Bekalli, we did so as heroes, with a heroic princess at our side and the grateful welcome of a reseated king. Sheroit dar Bontine lay dead, and a more deserving bastard never took a knife in the back from the hand of his one-time lover, a one-time queen. Jehan's conspiracy to rule all of Feyndala, and the murders of the young that had fueled it, fell under the bright light of day and lost strength and support, as much that is evil will when subjected to scrutiny.

Jerno found himself beloved, which in his best days before he had never been. He worked hard for the good of his people, and he remembered his obligation to Halleyne, too—he financed the carving of a cave along the tall cliffs of the seacoast, to be named Torassillavin, or the Cave

of Singing Winds, and named me advisor to the
engineers and craftsmen who began to build it.

Still, much remained undone. Jehan and his
children lived, and remained in power within their
realm. The *Driftwood* had not yet returned, and
Halleyne could not raise Shallia to discover its fate.

And last, but to the two of us most important
of all, our child grew bigger in Halleyne's belly
each day, and though she sang the spirits away
from him faithfully, and wore her ward, and visited
with her doctor as often as he requested and
sometimes oftener, we wondered how our infant
son would fare, and how we would fare with him.

But this notebook runs short of pages, and the tale
of Jehan and Teuper and Sora and our friends'
rescue from Landfall and the birth of our son—and
the part Halleyne and I played in all of it—is a tale
as tangled as a nest of Gloriana vipers, and long in
the telling. It must wait for another day and another
notebook. But when my hand is rested, and my
inkpot is refilled, and fresh pages lie before me, I
shall tell it. I promise.

> *By my hand and oath,*
> *Kin Underbridge*
> *Judge of Lieda and Byriver*